I0750109

Books by Corey Mesler:

Poetry

For Toby, Everything for Toby (1997) Wing & The Wheel Press
Ten Poets (1999) editor, only Wing & The Wheel Press
Piecework (2000) Wing & The Wheel Press
Chin-Chin in Eden (2003) Still Waters Press
Dark on Purpose (2004) Little Poem Press
The Hole in Sleep (2006) Wood Works Press
The Agoraphobe's Pandiculations (2006) Little Poem Press
The Lita Conversation (2006) Southern Hum
The Chloe Poems (2007) Maverick Duck Press
Some Identity Problems (2007) Foothills Publishing
Pictures from Lang and Fellini (2007) Sheltering Pines Press
Some Identity Problems (2008) Foothills Publishers
Grit (2008) Amsterdam Press

Prose

Talk: A Novel in Dialogue (2002) Livingston Press
We Are Billion-Year-Old Carbon (2005) Livingston Press
Short Story and Other Short Stories (2006) Parallel Press
Following Richard Brautigan (chapbook) (2006) Plan B Press
Publisher (chapbook) (2007) Workers Write Journal Press
Listen: 29 short Coversations (2009) Brown Paper Publishing
The Narcoleptic Therapists and Other Stories (2010) Achilles Chapbook Series

Following Richard Brautigan

Corey Mesler

LIVINGSTON PRESS
THE UNIVERSITY OF WEST ALABAMA

Copyright © 2010 Corey Meslet
All rights reserved, including electronic text
isbn 13: 978-1-60489-047-1 trade paper
Library of Congress Control Number 2009943939

Typesetting and page layout: Joe Taylor
Cover design and layout: Jennifer Brown
Cover photo: Eric Weber
Proofreading: Joe Taylor

The author would especially like to thank
John Barber and Eric Weber, whose support
for this project felt like sanctification.

This is a work of fiction.
Any resemblance to persons living or dead
or in-between is coincidence. Even those folks you think are real
are as phony as music mingling within a dream.

Livingston Press is part of The University of West Alabama, and
thereby has non-profit status.
Donations are tax-deductible:
brothers and sisters, we need 'em.

Following Richard Brautigan

"In watermelon sugar the deeds were done and done again as my life is done in watermelon sugar."

—Richard Brautigan

"His novels are off-beat, deliberately zany, completely different… People either love him or can't read him. The critical consensus might be summed up thus: he has more wit than wisdom."

—Martin Seymour-Smith

"On the cover of the recent record album, *Listening to Richard Brautigan*, … Brautigan is holding out his phone, as if inviting communication. You can call him up any time you want."

—Terence Malley

"I am yours
ghost and all."

—Richard Brautigan (from *June 30th, June 30th*)

this one is for my brother Mark for his sagacity and faith

ONE: A Quest

*A Barmy Ghost

I first began following Richard Brautigan in 1986. By this time, he had been dead for 2 years.

So, haunted, I was following a ghost, a barmy ghost first ensorcelled by the incandescence of a haunted decade called The Sixties, in an enchanted fiefdom called America, a place of libraries and trout streams, watermelon sugar and loco weed.

This is not fancy on my part. This ghost, the ghost of the writer Richard Brautigan, was as real as man's wonder, as solid as, as Mark Twain said, a gob of mud. And I followed, at first, out of fear and astonishment, and then, reader, out of love.

So, this, like many a tragedy before it, is a love story.

* My Name Is Jack

One normally comes to Richard Brautigan the same way one comes to the Beats. In early adulthood, when the world seems maladjusted and slightly off its axis. When the establishment, that you've been longing to deride, seems ready-made for ridicule, dadaism, revolt. These writers speak to young minds like spirits to mediums.

*My Name

Thus it was for me. I read *The Abortion* when I was 21. It became a very personal book for me, a totem, a talisman. I carried my little orange mass market paperback around with me as if in so doing I could transform myself from the moony, wispy, inconsequential struggling college student into a force for art and lunacy and holy hipsters and change.

In a way that little paperback created a new me. I quit college and got a job in a bookstore. I wanted to be a bohemian in the worst way. Forget that I came from the shitbox suburbs of a minor Mid-American city. Oklahoma City did not have a golden gate. It had an industrial decuman. I was on the bus. I was headed Further On.

My name is Jack.

*One's Need for the Quest, or Sir Galahad, Are You Really Taking Your Olivetti?

Next, I read *The Revenge of the Lawn*, a collection of short stories. But, were these short stories? They were certainly unlike anything I had come across in school. They had Hemingway's reticence and brevity but seemed to peter out before reaching a Hemingwayesque conclusion. They were witty and weird and made out of ticky-tack. In short, I loved them. And, in a way, I was thumbing my nose at my college professors, the ones who hadn't read a book published since 1945. The ones who made me read musty old dead men who told tales dripping with sense of place and character development. I admit: I was a nose thumber.

But that doesn't diminish Brautigan's appeal. His charm. He is one of the most charming, beguiling authors ever to put Olivet to foolscap. Bless his blond head, I thought.

And, of course, at this time Richard Brautigan was alive and, I thought, living in San Francisco, the birthplace of hippiedom, the home of City Lights Bookstore, a halidom, Mecca for radical readers. The truth was that he was all over the place: Montana, Japan, Nirvana. But I had him placed in San Francisco, and it was to San Francisco that I was to make my first adult journey, on a holy quest, with the zeal of a would-be poet and street-fighter.

*The Straight Line Was Called Interstate 40

By this time I had devoured all of Brautigan's books. The year was 1975. The year before I had taken another step on that shimmering stairway to adulthood: I had bought my first hardback book, *The Hawkline Monster*. It stamped my ticket. I had to travel. I had to find the roots of these works of wonder.

I was dewy-eyed. I was goony. And, worst of all, I was not a traveler.

I scrounged a map off my father—it was old enough that it said "Esso" on it, and this magic word: "Free." But it showed me something else, something that I took as a sign, at a time when I took many things as signs. There was a straight line between Oklahoma City and The West Coast. That straight line was called Interstate 40. It was new. It was virginal. It demanded that I climb aboard.

My parents took the news of my imminent departure with their customary incongruous hysteria.

"You can't just take off," my mother said, with the kind of finality one expected of life-changing pronouncements.

"Where will you stay?" my more practical father added.

"I'll find places," I said, unsure of myself, but sensing that this step—the denouncing of the pull of one's genitors—was an important one.

"You'll find places," my mother spat.

"What about your job?" my father asked.

"I've already asked Mrs. Tweedy. She said I could take a vacation, though I wouldn't qualify for a paid one for another six months."

"That's another thing. Money."

They had me there. I had very little money. I was drunk on the 60s. Money was evil, something gas companies created by raping the Mid-east, something bankers stacked up in their bedrooms to tantalize starlets. Filthy lucre.

Blood money. Or, as Freud, who I hadn't read at that time, would have it: shit.

"I was kind of hoping," I said, my emboldened Sweet Sir Galahad stance going limp, "that you would lend it to me."

Reader, they reluctantly agreed that I was old enough to make my own disasters. And my father pulled me aside—oh, sweet secret colloquy—and asked me how much I thought I needed.

*The Steering Wheel Felt Like a Dali Watch

The Steering wheel felt like a Dali watch. It seemed to melt in my hands. It would not stay upright, round, functional. I was dreaming.

It was the night before I was to leave.

I abandoned that rack of torture, the insomniac's bed, and took to the chair under the lamp in the den. There I re-read passages from *In Watermelon Sugar* and *The Pill Versus the Springhill Mining Disaster*. I studied the photographs on the covers. Brautigan. Kind-spirit.

The white night stretched out in front of me like a magic carpet. I was already traveling.

And though I worried that the lack of sleep might hinder my performance behind the wheel of a car, I was kissed by angels, the angels of whimsy, the angels of surrealism. Bookish angels!

And when dawn broke—an egg on a radiator—I was ready. I can do this, I said to myself, and myself answered, that's a pretty poor pep talk, but, hell, let's give it a shot.

*Charon, Steer Me Past L.A.

Oklahoma City, Las Vegas, Los Angeles, San Francisco.

The straight line that my imagination had created took me first to Los Angeles—I had to take a Bugs Bunny left to get to my ultimate destination. The City of Angels they call it. A great big freeway they call it.

I was happy to head toward Hippie Central. Los Angeles seemed Stygian to me. And when I first drove into SF I felt like a mariner touching land. But I was not a mariner—a buccaneer—but a footpad, a cross-country adventurer, a naïf. The city that opened before me like a book, a euchologion, was beautiful in its ramshackle, hilly recklessness. My heart gulped air like my carburetor. If a carburetor gulps air. I say it does.

I found a seedy hotel near Portrero Hill. I was sure Brautigan had mentioned Portrero Hill. It seemed a good augury. My first Brautigan-flash, an ur-epiphany. The gateway to later epiphanic synchronicity. This is the way my mind worked. Stay with me.

And when I threw my tired body down on that plywood bed I knew the exhilaration of the fortunate, the blessed. I was in San Francisco, in my own hotel room. I immediately let my mind go a-roaming, looking at the Maine-shaped water stain on the ceiling and in it seeing the face of every woman I had ever wanted.

It was a rite of passage. My propylaeum to adulthood.

The saintly ostiary waved me by.

*The Map of Me

My name is Jack.

My name is Jack and I am in San Francisco, the same city where Richard Brautigan resides. Or so I believe.

Do I expect to run into him on the street?

Do I expect to stop him and say, "Richard Brautigan, you are more than the sum of your parts; you are a special piece of my personal geography, the map of me?

Why am I here?

Why is anyone?

Why is anyone?

*Some Reference Material Enters the Story

'There are reasons why writers who write a lot, as Rudyard (Kipling) did, have big appetites. They are dancing bundles of desire. Writers who write crave sex, peanuts, and Nobel Prizes. They crave; they itch; they lust; they are alive. Whether they manage this mélange of desires well is a separate matter. But without this dancing, pressing desire they would sit quietly like old folks lined up in the corridor of a nursing home. Honor your goal to create a world by burning with desire. Be incandescent - or nothing will happen"

—Eric Maisel, from *A Writer's San Francisco*

*Antigone's Jockstrap

So, on my first day in San Francisco I go where any literary hobo would go, to The Promised Land. To City Lights Bookstore.

And there I am as comfortable as a dog in Lent.

Immediately, I imbibe the atmosphere of the place, like reading the ancient texts through breathing in the smoke of them burning. There is a poetry magazine wall!

And, there on that poetry magazine wall is a small poetry magazine called *Antigone's Jockstrap*.

And in *Antigone's Jockstrap* is a small poem called, "School's Out."

And the poet's name is Jack, the same as mine.

Did I mention that I write poetry?

Because it is my poem, accepted by this peculiar little magazine about a month before.

I am as if sanctified.

I hold the magazine up and look around me—am I about to exclaim publicly? A man in a soiled, floor-length duster, which seems crazy indeed in summer, looks at me like I'm Rod McKuen. I put *Antigone's Jockstrap* back in its place and grin sheepishly.

This is Day One, not counting the meal I ate at a Vietnamese restaurant in Chinatown—Hot and Sour Catfish Soup, Bun Cha Gio, a cool Tsing Tao.

It was a good meal and I thanked my waiter a tad profusely.

***Mr. Ferlinghetti**

The second day in San Francisco I return to City Lights Bookstore. I'm beginning to lose the sense of purpose which sent me westward.

I browse the poetry shelves. It's a whole world, a miniature world, black marks on paper, but, nevertheless, a world as ripe as ass's milk. It's where I want to live.

I go back upstairs. Did I mention there are two levels to City Light's Bookstore? Do I need to?

There's a bohemian manning the cash register. Of course there is. He looks like he is a jazz musician. I'm intimidated with my Oklahoma City accent and my hippie clothes bought at J.C. Penney's. I imagine he sees through me.

I make bold.

I ask him, "Um, does Mr. Ferlinghetti come in often?"

He answers me as if I am a human being. This is kind of

him.

"He normally comes in about this time to check the mail."

"Mm," I say, as if that is of minor interest to me. "Thank you."

I return to the poetry shelves where I find a small Frank O'Hara. Frank O'Hara makes me happy. He can make me happy on the bleakest of days. I read: "Is your throat dry with the deviousness of following?"

This quote will reveal its import later, like a tiny timebomb in my psyche.

Upstairs I hear Mr. Ferlinghetti's vivid voice. I grab a copy of his *Selected Poems* off the shelf and scuttle up the stairs.

Once out of the depths I gasp for air. Mr. Ferlinghetti hasn't noticed me yet—he didn't see my precipitate and foolish dash.

"Hello," I manage.

He looks up.

"Hi," he says. He looks like The Cat in the Hat if The Cat in the Hat were the godfather of beat poetry.

"Would you mind signing this?" I ask him. I hand him his own book. "And I'll buy it," I think to add, just in case they think I am a scofflaw. But, perhaps, a part of me whispers, scofflaws are honored here.

"What's your name?"

"Jack."

"Where you from, Jack?"

"Oklahoma."

"What brings you to San Francisco?"

I'm doing alright. I'm holding my own.

"Holy quest," I say, with a trace of irony.

"Ah," Lawrence Ferlinghetti says and hands the paperback book back to me.

"Thank you," I say.

"Good luck," Lawrence Ferlinghetti says.

Back out on the street I open the book. He has written, "For Jack, who knows a good quest when he sees one."

I am consecrated.

I go back to Chinatown for dinner.

***The Sky Is a Sheet of Foolscap**

On the third day I begin my quest for Richard Brautigan in earnest.

I head to People's Park.

The day is like a young girl, milk and roses. The sky is a sheet of foolscap. There are young people everywhere, women in silks and little else.

Every glimpse of midriff is a razor across my heart.

Still my heart expands.

I can't take my eyes off one gypsy-woman, dancing with a tambourine to a song played on a recorder by her lover, an Ian Anderson look-alike, even down to his dirty raincoat. She gyrates and swirls, Ezmeralda, Salomé.

And that is when I have a vision.

There's an old woman on a park bench, muttering to herself, clad in an abundance of castoff raiments, too much clothing for so temperate a day. She holds in her hand a book.

As I pass her she looks up. Her face is suddenly young, beautiful. It is the face of Joan of Arc. She is Joan of Arc.

I stop. I look at her book. It's a pornographic novel called *Jill's Gangbang.*

Joan of Arc fixes me with a fiery eye.

I am in love. My trousers stiffen. She reaches out her hand toward the bulge in my middle self…

And I woke up back in my hotel room. The clock said 4:35. I was starving.

I sat up.

My pants were around my ankles and there was dried come on my belly.

And on the third day he rose…

*The Absence of Richard Brautigan and the Franz Kline Shirt

Time is passing and I realize I am no closer to Richard Brautigan than I was back in Oklahoma City. On the fourth day I begin to ask strangers if they know how to contact Richard Brautigan.

I wander the streets, lonely as a crowd.

I eat a gyro sandwich I buy from a small café, the cucumber sauce dripping onto my shirt front as I walk. After I finish eating I try to rub my shirt clean with the Kleenex-size napkin they provided. I make a smear that looks something like a Franz Kline painting.

I walk back to City Lights Bookstore. I am getting nowhere.

I bolster myself and ask the beatnik clerk if he knows where I can find Richard Brautigan. I understand that I am as foolish as a beetlehead.

He says, “Yeah. I think he’s in Japan.”

“Really?” I ask, trying not to sound twelve years old.

“I believe so,” he says.

“Hm,” I say, as if I had an appointment with him and he has disappointed me.

“Anything else?” he asks. He’s sort of half-smiling so I’m not sure if he wants me to move on or not.

“Uh, no.”

“Ok.” He goes back to his copy of *The Village Voice*.

“Oh, do you know where his house is? The one in San Francisco?” I’m slipping away.

“Sure.”

“Ok,” I say.

“Ok,” he says, too.

“See ya.”

“Yep.”

***How Richard Brautigan Was (Is)**
a Conduit of Pure Love and Pure Destruction

After I left City Lights bookstore I felt a bit down. My shirt smelled and my quest was fizzling.

I am walking down Columbus when I see her.

She is reading *Revenge of the Lawn* and swaying toward me on the sidewalk. She seems practiced in reading and walking at the same time. It’s not easy. Try it some time.

She was (is) as lovely as a fairy dancing in a sunbeam.

She has chocolate colored hair and freckles and her body

moves with the grace of an ocelot. She was (is) lithe. She was (is) willowy.

"Ah, Brautigan," I try as she draws nigh.

She looks up. Her eyes were (are) grey. She stops my heart.

"Yes," she says.

"I loved that one," I say.

She looks at her book as if she can't remember what she is reading.

"Uh huh," she says.

We stand at an impasse. A great gulf opens up between us and if I do not bridge it quickly she will diminish like a morning's frost.

"I—" I begin.

"You're not from here," she breaks in.

My accent. Hick, is what she's thinking.

"Right," I say. "Oklahoma City."

"Ah."

"Right."

"Well."

"Jack," I say, and stick out my hand.

She stares at me for a second. Is this a knife I see before me? She is unsure. She wants to fix me like a photograph.

"Sharilyn."

I don't take it in. I am lost in her eyes.

"Hm?" I say.

"Like Marilyn with an S. Or Sh. My parents," she says and shrugs.

"Lovely" I say.

She laughs a quick laugh, almost a bark.

"Really? Sharilyn?"

"You," I say. I don't know where it came from.

She hesitates a heartbeat. Then she beams.

"I've never been called lovely before."

"You should have been. Every day." I have a tendency to go too far, too fast. I reined in.

"My, aren't you, what? flirtatious?"

"Do you want to get a cup of coffee?"

Again the heartbeat.

"Sure," she says. "I'm on lunchbreak."

"Ok," I say.

"You have a Franz Kline smear on your shirt," she says.

***A Difficult Name, an Enchantment**

It turned out she worked in publishing, for this firm that specialized in handsomely produced volumes, with little text, but gorgeous artwork. The kind of book you gave to your hip aunt. Almost a coffee table book, but not quite. A little funkier than that. This was their forte, their raison d'etre. They had cornered the market on funky chic.

Her full name was, is, Sharilyn Chwedyk. A difficult name, an enchantment, the secret word the elves bestow to enter their sovereignty.

In that 33 minutes we had together we made a connection. Who can say why it works sometimes and sometimes it does not? The world is agley and humans mere corks on the sea.

We made a date for that night.

In a way we had to work in double-time. We had to speed things up. I wasn't in San Francisco forever.

That night we went to a small art theater, the kind of place I had only read about, the kind of thing Oklahoma City wouldn't know what to do with. A movie theater on the side of a large carnival house, run by a couple who lived above it.

The movie was Godard's *Alphaville.* I love *Alphaville.*

But I could not concentrate. I wanted only to kiss Sharilyn Chwedyk.

And, friends, I did. Later, after the movie, leaning against the wall of my hotel, in the waning hours of that day. She had driven me back to my hotel in her Volkswagen. I loved that she drove a Volkswagen. I love(d) much about Sharilyn Chwedyk.

And when I held her—it was that kind of kiss—her willowy body felt like love's last best song. A twining vine. The kiss went on and on. It held promise, futurity, velleities.

We made plans to meet after she got off work the next day.

We were going to Chinatown for dinner.

*She Was Peppery with Freckles, a Paphian Tangle

I summarize:

It's after dinner. We are at her apartment. The kind of apartment you can afford if you live in San Francisco and work for a small publisher. But decorated with taste and just the right dollop of strangeness.

There was a poster of the actress, Jean Seberg, as Joan of Arc.

Joan of Arc.

There was a large, knitted Ojo.

There was a cat named Pudding.

There was a couch, as soft as a daydream, upon which she bent backward to receive my kiss and hands. A couch upon which we unclothed and felt along the wayward lines of each other's body.

She took me firmly in her hand. Her grip was strong—she had thin, firm hands, tapered fingers, peppery with freckles. She moved me up and down as expertly as I could do myself.

I knelt to place my mouth upon her moistened middle. She flushed deeply, her chest a quick and bright mottle, a celestial, roseate flame.

"Oh my," she said.

And when I entered her it was as if we had been lovers for all time, Ulysses and Penelope, Pyramus and Thisbe, William Powell and Myrna Loy.

Sharilyn Chwedyk moved underneath me like a snake, her skin fresh like a freshet. Sharilyn Chwedyk sat upon me like faith's hue, moving her surprisingly ample bottom—up until then disguised by her hippie dresses—the way the wind moves the waves.

And, believe this or don't: we came simultaneously. Our howls commingling in perfect harmony.

Lennon and McCartney.

I fell so hard, friends. I fell so far.

James Joyce said, "First we feel. Then we fall."

This is the story I wish to tell.

Richard Brautigan became unreal to me that night. Even as *Revenge of the Lawn* lay splayed like a broken bird on the coffee table nearby.

We looked at each other. We recognized something. Perhaps you who have been there have a name for it.

Her body shone like ambergris beside me. And, reader, excuse this indiscretion: Sharilyn had the wettest, prettiest sex I'd ever touched, kissed, sucked. She ran like the world's first rivers. I still relished its kinship with damp loam, as we lay in the aftermath, sticky with humors.

"I hardly know what to say," I said.

"I don't either," she said.

"May I stay the night?" I asked, a courtier.

She smiled and my heart went ka-chunk.

"Yes, you may," she said.

She stood up and I sat still for a moment so that I could watch her walk away. Her underside was a prothalamion. She was as sexy as a fire.

"Come on," she said.

I stood up.

"Oh, wait," I said.

I turned back and picked up *Revenge of the Lawn* and placed a magazine subscription form in it as a bookmark. It was no longer a wounded bird. It was the charm which brought me together with Sharilyn Chwedyk.

***Sharilyn**

"Strap yourself to the tree with roots.
You ain't going nowhere."
Bob Dylan

Consider the silence in the
stillness, the silence
of music, of two hearts

rubbed together. There is

strength and austerity
and the sturdy sophistic
stillness of the silence.
It is in the unreasoning that
we bloom, the silent
together.

I write this to a strange woman
I've never met, hoping my words
will make her love me.
We are all lonely in the face of
what we have to say, even if
we have nothing to say.

*I Fall Into Sharilyn Chwedyk the Way Small Birds Beaten by the Storm Fall

I had three more days in San Francisco. Thoughts of the hippie-surrealist writer whose writings had brought me west immerged like dew. I was retted with this foxy, slender woman, whose every movement seemed to me to embody a smoldering sexuality. Sharilyn, who is both dark and light—chocolate hair and skin like sea foam. And those freckles—they were a map to her soul, to my soul, to the linking of two souls. Do I overspeak? No.

Favorite memory of those first heady days: well, the sex, of course. Who, honestly would say otherwise?

Also: the day we spent driving all over that transcendent city, whose surface is like a rumpled counterpane, in search of used books. There are as many used bookstores in San Francisco as there are churches, or so it seemed to me on that magickal day.

Am I misremembering this? There was one called An Unclean Dimly Lit Place for Books? In which I found a paperback of *Tarzan of the Apes*, a book I'd always meant to read—I know, it's not exactly Thomas Mann. But therein I found this gem of a line: "Tarzan began to hold his own kind in but low esteem."

Other memorable bargains from that cornucopia of literature: a cheap first edition of Peter Devries' delightful *Reuben, Reuben*. A trade paperback of Tanizaki's *The Key*. A nice hardback of *A Coffin for Dimitrios*. Sharilyn bought a fine Modern Library of *Six Plays by Ibsen*.

And to keep on track: I splurged on a first edition of *In Watermelon Sugar*. The same dealer—I can't remember which, though I think it was either Books by the Bay, or The Republic of Letters—had a *Please Plant this Book*, with all seed packets attached, but my wallet would not allow.

And all the while, by my side, smiling enthusiasm and warmth, the willowy, the pluvial Sharilyn Chwedyk.

Who reads Ibsen.

*There Are Angels in the Postal Service

Who said all good things come to an end? Who was the first man to utter this jail sentence, this sword of Damocles, under which humankind has labored for centuries?

No.

We would not let it end.

When we parted, in the airport terminal (terminal, friend) it was with rich promises and hungry kisses. There was the telephone, the angels in the postal service, and, hope against hope, the occasional flight between Oklahoma City (weak, dead fizgig end) and San Francisco (The Garden).

We would stay together through stubborn insistence, through passion. It was meant to be. This is how we felt.

TWO: The Letters

*Whimsyland and *Little, Big*

"And so because he had no choice, Smoky sat down to make love through the mails with a thoroughness just about vanished from the world," John Crowley writes in his supernal fantasy novel, *Little, Big*. Can humans live in fantasy?

Yes, they can.

It takes faith. It takes obdurate will. It takes a little of the wonky magic one finds in novels by Richard Brautigan. This is how I began to see it. We were living in Richard Brautigan whimsyland.

*Sex-Memory and Caffeine

And so, fueled by sex-memory and caffeine, we began our correspondence. My first letter went something like this:

Dear Sharilyn, my Shar,

Only a few days separate us, yet I'm completely discombobulated by your absence. I feel like an addict coming off smack, though I have no idea how an addict coming off smack would feel.

When I arrived home I expected a pile of mail, like you see in the movies, when the returning hero steps into his foyer onto a sliding mass of letters and cards and circulars, a veritable Everest of correspondence in need of answer. There was one letter from the place where I bought my car. There was one card from a friend who is in Prague: a shot of one of Kafka's houses. There was an ad sheet from the grocery store down the street: rump roasts are apparently going for rock-bottom prices.

In my fervid imagination I half-expected a letter from you waiting for me, though I knew this was foolish since you would have had to send it before I actually left you.

So, I write today, full of you, full of submissiveness and starlight, wanting words on paper for you to hold and cherish and run your fingers across, knowing their reality, their red-brick substantiality. Even though I plan on calling you tonight. Phone sex is not real sex but it's better than no sex. Right?

I'm rambling—you'll get this after we've talked. After we've experimented with the first phone sex—will it work? Will we be shy on that strange communication device, that plastic receiver which I don't believe in? Why is it called a "receiver?" Wouldn't "sender/receiver" be more to the point? Will we be able to put into words the passion we experienced on your couch, in your bed, and that one time in your cramped Volkswagen?

Ah, that cramped Volkswagen sex. That was a trick worthy of Houdini. How is it that your legs folded that way, as if you were some faultless device, some cleverly designed piece of holy workmanship? Car sex is normally just oral sex—am I right?—yet we managed to make it all the way, make it work all the way. When you sat on me I thought the top of my head might come off.

Leonard Cohen:

"Come down to my rooms
I was thinking about you
and I made a pass at myself."

If we even need to recount our minutia. And perhaps couples do—perhaps that is part of the glue. Do we have glue, My Shar, are we a couple? I wonder.

We will talk about this and many other things.

love, for now,
Your Jack

Dear Jack, my Jackoff,

I got your letter and wanted to write right back. Yes, since receiving it we have talked on the phone—how many times? 12? –it seems to me an amazing number. And we have had our phone sex a concomitant number of times.

How your voice caresses me. I can feel your breath on me, on my stomach, over my breasts. And when you say, I kiss your inner thigh, I can feel that, too, and your warm mouth over my warmer sex, so wet with your words, your wily ways. Too much alliteration, sorry, it's the poet in me. The woman who wants to be a poet.

Now you know my dirtiest secret—and it's not that I love to suck you—but that I want to be a poet. Oh, Jack, I'm not good enough. I send these things out, these Diana DiPrima imitations, these faux Anne Sextons, and they always come back, with crappy little slips of paper snuggled up next to them in the envelope, form rejection notes that they couldn't even waste a full sheet of paper on. Sorry to whine about this—I am writing poems about you, about us, and I guess, in a way, I want you to know, but I don't think I can show them to you. They do not do justice to your boyish smile, your undulate hair, your beautiful beautiful cock.

I'm closing this letter fast, now my Jack, because I've told you something precious and I have to sit back and think about whether I am going to send it. If you're reading this it means my wrestling with myself went your way—this will show you the trust I have in you, in us.

Ach, I'm going to call you. I need to touch myself while you tell me sweet things.

love and tender kisses,
your Sharilyn

Dear Shar, my poetess,

I've argued with you enough about this. You must send me some poetry. Send me something not about me to start, if that would make it easier. I want your words, all your words, the ones you keep locked up, the ones you would only show your last, best lover. I want to be that—your last, best lover. Am I too impetuous? Do I push too soon? I have that tendency—please don't let me. Don't let me make the space between us uncomfortable.

I don't want space between us.

I want you right up against me, your breath in my ear, urging me on. My memory is saturated with sex with you. I can't remember my mother's maiden name, or the name of the guy down on the corner who stands there every day with his dog and waves at the traffic. One of Oklahoma City's colorful characters.

If you won't show me your poems I won't show you my, um, darker side. Ok, that's an empty threat. I have no darker side. How about this? If you will send me one poem I will tell you why I was in San Francisco. Isn't that funny? You never asked.

I have to close now and work on the store's newsletter. We're trying our first full-color insert and I have to pick the books to include and write a little squib about each. I'm thinking of maybe doing a Beat Poets section, but I don't think the owner will go for it. Full-color means money, so I'm guessing I'm supposed to pick high-end items. There's a glossy book about The Beatles due out—

and I think an Abrams book on Marc Chagall.
This is boring. This bores.
I kiss your inner thigh.

lovelovelove,
your erstwhile and future lover,
Jack

O Jack,

For V.W., with Exaggeration

I'll have an entendre,
make it a double.
The things I used to not
fathom I can now stand
for short periods.
An ellipsis of the moon,
phases I recall from
Bartlett's, or maxims
we learned at lunch.
All these things seem to
me now to be glittering
spectacles, glasses
to be seen through darkly.
On the plain face of it
I guess a word or two
here and there can pep
me up. But, you, with
your wit and your backhand

are not courtly or wise.
I refute your reputation.
I resist your moony pull.
I sit up now and take
notice, twice daily,

with the rest of the barbiturates.
Then I lie, down
like poor Virginia, after a
novel. Death to all
tyrants, amends to all whom
I have armed. And, in
the end, nothing but love,
that empty vessel, that
primaveral pop to my step,
that slap-in-the-face freshet.

sheepishly, shy suddenly,
(alliteration all anxiety ascending)
your Sharilyn always

Dear Grand Poetess, my Forever Love,

As I stated on the phone, your poem is dynamite, something other, something fey is in it, something from deep within you. I don't quite know how to talk about it.

And as I promised on the phone I will now tell you what I was doing in San Francisco: I was looking for Richard Brautigan.

Literally.

Sometime in the last half year, maybe year, I developed this fixation on that whimsical genius, with the hippie head and the pen full of peris. I thought—and this is crazy—I thought if I could meet him, talk to him, I would be somehow blessed—no, that's too fancy a word. I would be released from his spell somehow, free to be myself, my whole self for the first time. I'm explaining this badly. I'm overstating things.

Perhaps it's just a cannabis delusion.

Anyway, we both know what happened. I found you instead. Like Christopher Columbus ("The petals of the vagina unfold/like Christopher Columbus/taking off his shoes") I found something better and all thoughts of Richard Brautigan went out of my head. Now, back at home, he has returned, but only as a shadowy presence, a spirit who looks over my shoulder as I write this letter.

And, another confession, I write poetry, too.

And I have love poems to you. Do I dare share them? I will if you will. I'll show you mine if you'll show me yours.

Which now has me thinking of your beautiful crotch, which has a scent like mushrooms and champagne, and which is wet like loam. I suck there as the bee sucks, or whatever it is that Emily Dickinson said, though I doubt she was talking about oral sex. Or perhaps she was. Meat for a thesis, yes?

Hell, why be coy? Here's a poem I wrote about you 2 days ago. Perhaps I should spend more time on it, polish it until it's perfect like you, but, no, I want you to feel the raw desire behind it. Ok? This means we send poems back and forth, ok? This begins it.

A Flower

If I tell you she has a flower
where her crotch should be
you might look away, just this once.
But I confess: wanton and hyperbolic,
she undressed in front of the

TV. She has a flower where her crotch
should be. Should it be just
a flower, I'm down on my knees, a
flower, a flower, where her crotch should be.
Should be, should be, and me
apropos of nothing, going down,
on my knees in abeyance to the miracle girl,
who has a flower, a sweet spring flower
mind you, where her crotch should be.

now I'm really thinking about you,
and sealing this with a kiss—for your inner thigh,
Jack

Dear Jack-o-lantern,

You write poetry, you love, you dear. And you're so sweet about mine. I include here four more poems for you to peruse and let me know what you think. The one called "Sex Anamnesis" is, of course, about you. You are my devil doll, my little sex toy. I want to pull you apart and put you back together with my mouth.

Wait, that's not bad. I'm gonna rework that line into a poem, I think.

Things at the press are in an uproar. Apparently, this last quarter was way below expectations and everyone is walking around as if they had skins of glass. Cutbacks are being talked about, though I don't know by whom. I should be safe, if only because my job description is so vague that no one else would know how to begin it. I am the Jack of all Trades around here. A Jack like you, though I may be the One-Eye, while you have two eyes and perfect vision. You are a perfect vision.

(Yet, as we know, I love my little oneeyedjack, too.)

I can't tell you how much it means to me to have you praise my poor trifling poems. I'm still having no luck placing them at all. Big Table just sent a batch back with a scribbled note on the bottom, "Please send only your best stuff."

Ouch.

I thought I was. At least I got a scribbled note. Does this mean that they saw something in the poems I sent them—even though they disliked them—that showed promise? I don't know. I grow weary trying to figure out what editors mean, if they mean anything. Sometimes I feel like they comment just because in that way they feel like editors. They are playing at being editors.

Maybe I'm shooting too high. Should I start with smaller rags? With magazines with readerships in the single digits? Like Antigone's Jockstrap. Like Cum. I'm not kidding—these are rags I've seen around town. Perhaps I just need a few credits.

Does all this talk bore you? Does my ambitious nature turn you off, you who say you don't want to send your poems out into the world? And why don't you, my sweet? It would help me to know that you were chancing the same choppy waters I'm chancing. I won't nag.

And knowing what I know now...I could send you a photo of my familiar—but I'm not sure how interested you are in a photo of me pleasing myself.

Ahhh...your poetry is soft yet potent music between my thighs...if you only knew about the spectrum of inner thoughts inside the ripe womanly flesh .

My crotch smarts for you. It is smart enough to know you and want you. Imagine me looking at your cock right now. Yum.

love, your horny Shar
(the lion's share?)

Dear dear Shar,

Forget those rags and their cranky editors. Your stuff—as evidenced by these new poems you've sent—is idiosyncratic and delightful. It's gonna take a smart reader to appreciate them—and there simply aren't that many smart readers out there, on magazine staffs or elsewhere. The poem to me I have tacked above my own writing desk—my escritoire—to inspire me. It touches me so deeply, as I told you on the phone—I'm too close to it to judge its literary value but, given your gift, I will confidently and with great pride declare it a work of art.

And the others—where did you come from, inscrutable woman? You're like some dark grimalkin—a witch's cat, witchy, diabolic and as sexy as a feline. I love the phrase,

"There's
just enough magic left
in the sunset for a quick sestina."

Keep writing, my love, my best and last flame. You are the sun and the moon and all the attendant stars. I kiss you—here, there and everywhere.

I'm enclosing a dozen poems. Forgive my overflow. I am ginned by your talent, your love, your willingness to share the most private part of you.

Woman, you have me wrapped around your little finger, or any other body part you would wish. May I have a picture of you pleasuring yourself? My God in Heaven.

I'll make it a holy object. And I will worship also the person within. Send me visuals—-in any form. You sensual, beautiful, breath of sea air disguised as a female.

I'm already hypnotized.

Richard Brautigan: "We went over and lay upon the bed. I took her dress off. She had nothing on underneath. We did that for a while. Then I got up and took off my overalls and lay back down beside her."

I want to "do that for a while.'

Cock-a-Hoop
for Sharilyn

Your mouth on me like a poem.
Your slim backside bent over
me like a poem. Your sweet vaginal
lips in my mouth like a poem.
And afterwards the holycow feeling
of just being human and
satisfied like a goddamn poem.

your Jack-of-few-trades

Dear Jackbenimble,

O your new poems! Are they new? I know the one about me must be new. Am I really "inside your chest/like another heart"? O my Jack. You are a man of complexity and sexiness and all-around humanbeinggoodness. I love you, my Jackbenimble!

Layoffs at the press yesterday. Damnation! We talked about this but I'm not letting it go. They fired Lynda, my best friend! Those bastards. I'd walk if I didn't need this shitty job so much. And Lynda, just getting divorced, trying to win her custody battle with her inattentive, bloodless husband, just getting her own place—the whole thing makes me sick. Last night I went to visit her—and missed your call! O fie and damnation!—and she and Nora were eating macaroni and cheese on this rickety little table that looks like it was made out of cheap pipes and leftover linoleum—and it was just so fucking sad, Jack. Little Nora—you should see her, five years old and as full of wisdom as a little Buddha—she asked me if I was going to live with them. She asked me if I was going to be her new dad. I cried.

Sorry to go on in such a depressing vein.

I'll switch gears.

Or maybe I should end here and throw in some more poems. By the by, my favorite of this last batch—well, I have many, but will only name one for now—is "Bethlehem Holiday Inn." You write little stories with your poems, something that would never occur to me to do. Clever, clever Jack.

Don't let the mood of this letter enter your bloodstream.

I love you with a fierce brightness.

lovely life-enhancing love,

your Shar

PS: I found this word last night in a book I was reading, probably you already know it, since little boys are so penis-proud. Pizzle. I want your pizzle, your big, bull-sized pizzle.

Dear Shar-of-my-Heart,

Your last letter was a downer. And I haven't been able to reach you on the phone except for that one night that Lynda was there. I know you've been taking care of her—my big-hearted Sharilyn—but, damn, I miss you. I miss our phone sex. I need it and will try again tonight. Please be there. Well, by the time you get this we will surely have had phone sex again and all will be well with the world.

Don't think that I don't care about your friend and her travails. I do. Truly, I do. What you love, I love. Ok?

Of your new poems: what a wily kitty you are! I love "Frozen Aunt Jemima" and "Love at the Speed of Light." These are highly publishable. Are you still sending stuff out? Don't give up—don't especially just because your feckless boyfriend is too timid or insular or whatever I am to send stuff out. I don't need editors telling me, "Send only your best stuff." Bastards.

But you, you should be widely disseminated like the polio vaccine.

I'm gonna stop here, walk this to the corner box—it's a crisp, cool evening, the kind we get occasionally in this godless city, a hint of seasonal change in the air like a balm—and send it to you, along with these five poems, four of which are brand new and perhaps need a polish. You will be honest with me and tell me what to correct, won't you, my perspicacious poetess.

Are you still planning to send me a sexy photograph? It sure would help me. I would set it up—like Laura's portrait in *Laura*—and worship it as if it were my own private halidom, which it would be. And then I'm going to call you so you can whisper in my ear: pizzle.

a neck-breaking love,
Jack

Dear Jack,

Sorry I haven't been around to take your calls. Things aren't that great here. I think I may have depression, you know? like clinical depression. I can barely make it to work—and of course work is such a crappy place to be right now.

I liked your last poems. I do think they need a polish. Is

the line "I wanted to fuck all the pretty girls" really necessary? Is it poetry?

I'm feeling bitchy.

I better stop.

love,
Sharilyn

Dear Sharilyn, my Sharilyn,

When we talked on the phone Wednesday I thought you sounded tired—is it just depression? Have you thought about going to the doctor, maybe a shrink? I'm not ragging on you, but I hate to hear my sparkling nymph sound so dragged out and unhappy.

I did enjoy the sex talk—even if it were just for me. You can make me come with your kittycat voice. But, you didn't want reciprocation and that wasn't as satisfying.

I'm gonna enclose a dozen poems here—in hopes that you like this batch better than the last. Perhaps, you're right—although I'm childish and stubborn and it hurt to hear you say a certain line didn't seem like poetry to you. That's just my insecurity. I'll take a harder look at that poem. These that I'm including today are ones I've written over the past year, and there's one for you, as there always is. I'm sure you can figure out which.

The bookstore is putting undue pressure on me to "maximize sales." I hate this kind of talk and don't want to hear it in the book business, which I'm just romantic enough to think is still a gentle, even eccentric business. Frank, the owner, (Mrs. Tweedy is his wife, really just a figurehead like the Queen) has even talked of putting the clerks—Tammy, Kate and even me—on some kind of commission. Oh, please. I may have to look elsewhere for employment—there's an antiquarian bookstore downtown that may be hiring. I don't know squat about old books but I'm a fast learner.

Reading Alice Hoffman's *Illumination Night*, which I'm liking as much as *Seventh Heaven*, which was sterling.

I'm rambling—just to keep your attention, I think.

Picture?

I'll close with kisses and caresses and my mouth wandering your hilly curves.

yr hot boytoy,
Jackoff

Dear Jack,

You're expending an awful amount of emotional energy on me. Am I worth it? Do you really want to throw your love in a hole? No, that's too harsh, but let it be a signal as to my current state, that I'm leaving the question here.

I liked your most recent batch of poems.

If I can ever look at my work again I'll send you something.

I gotta go. There's a guy from a local arts magazine coming over to interview me. Don't ask why.

Love,
Sharilyn

Dear Shar,

I can't get you on the phone. I'm dying here. I physically

ache for you.

Listen: I'm thinking about coming out to San Francisco—maybe before the holidays start and things get really busy at the store. I think Frank would let me go—he may even relish my going. I think I'm a thorn in his moneygrubbing side.

What do you say? I can fly out on a Thursday night and leave on Sunday night. It would give us 3 glorious nights together.

Here's a new poem I wrote for you.

For Sharilyn, Because It Went by So Fast

"I loved you for your beauty
but that doesn't make a fool of me."
—Leonard Cohen

Her glances could break arms.
Her hair was a nimbus
of tangled nestings,
life surrounded her like a cloak.
When I went too deep
she was quick to pull the plug.
I still stay awake nights
reliving the ignominy, forgetting
to celebrate how we came
together briefly, fiery angels.

I will call you to discuss travel plans.
I love you.
Jack

Dear Jack,

It was good to talk to you on the phone. Sorry, Jerry

was here—that's the guy from the magazine—did I tell you that already?

Anyway, things here are nuts—they always seem to be these days. I used to hate people who always seemed too busy to give you their full attention—I always thought, hell, no one is that busy. But, I think I've turned into one of those people.

Spent the night at Lynda's last night—why I missed your call.

I'll see you Thursday night.

Love,
Sharilyn

***The Cloth Raincoat and the Nothing Hand Grenade**

So, I packed a bag, friends, and I flew to San Francisco. The sky in Oklahoma City, when I left, was the color of a frying pan, a dirty frying pan.

When I landed in San Francisco, the sky was the color of a frying pan. It was the same damn sky.

Sharilyn met me at the airport. She was dressed in a cloth raincoat, long-sleeved jersey, corduroy pants. She didn't look sexy. She looked purposely unsexy. But, I'm getting ahead, projecting.

The mouth she offered me for a kiss was dry. The embrace clumsy.

We drove to her apartment.

It was almost 10:30 when we arrived. I put my bag in her room and went back out to the living room, where she sat on the couch. The Couch.

Her face was set, her smile a weak approximation.

"What is it?" I asked, pointedly, as I sat. Up until then I had endured the near silent car ride, the shitty small talk, the one word answers.

"Nothing," she said. It was the kind of nothing that tunnels into your heart, the nothing that rocks a world. Some people hand out these kinds of nothings like alms. It's like she presented me with a hand grenade, with the pin pulled, and said, here, sweet, be careful, this is Nothing.

***The Nothing Tunnels Further Into My Heart**

We went to bed. I stripped down to my briefs. She wore pajamas, which were either seductive or sloppy, depending on how you are on the history of human relations.

She presented her back to me and I pulled up against her.

My hardon in her crack. She couldn't have missed it.

"Jack," she said.

"Yes, sweet," I tried. It was a pitiful retort. Pity me.

"I don't think we should. Tonight."

Did that "tonight" portend future couplings?

"What's wrong, Shar?"

"It's nothing. It's just me. This is the me I was trying to warn you about. The crazy one. You can't love a crazy person, Jack."

I thought about that for a minute.

"Is it someone else, Shar? Is it that magazine writer, Jeff?'

"Jerry."

"Right."

"No."

"No, it's not Jerry, or no there's not anybody else."

"The latter. It's not anybody, Jack."

"Have you slept with anyone else, Shar?"

She hesitated and in that hesitation a multitude of stars burned out, forever.

"Lynda," she said, finally.

"Well, I know…" I said. You have to believe me when I say that I thought nothing of this.

"Can we just go to sleep?" she asked. "Tomorrow, maybe I'll be better."

***The Quicksand Legions of History**

Tomorrow was no different.

Unless you count a listless handjob before we slept as better. She said she didn't feel like being touched herself, but, she knew that I was looking forward to sex, so…

She said she didn't want to be touched. That she felt unclean.

I have no idea what this means.

I didn't then and I don't now.

After the handjob, she kissed me, a slightly moister kiss than the one at the airport but not the kind of kiss one pins hopes upon.

The next night I slept on the couch.

Sunday afternoon, after a lunch in Chinatown, she drove me to the airport.

“I’m sorry,” she said. “I’ll make it up to you.” She gave me another airport kiss.

I was three hours early for my flight.

My flight felt like someone was pulling out my vital organs, slowly, like taffy. A long, deliberate *mittelschmerz.*

My apartment had a ghost in it.

I was a ghost.

*It’s Raining in Goddamn

Soon she stopped answering the phone and my letters.

I would call and the phone would ring and ring, its sound dopplering away, like the turning over of the Confederate dead.

Then, later, the recorded voice, a voice like the voice of a witch who had been stripped of her power: the number you need has been disconnected. Please check the number and try again.

I checked. I tried. Again and again and again.

And my letters were met with quash. My letters got lost along the way, the children of birds. They said nothing and their ink faded, faded and was gone. Lemon juice writing.

She stopped answering me. Who has that kind of power?

Then the first letter came back with “Moved/no forwarding address.” Then the next letter the same.

I ask you: who has that kind of power?

THREE: The Next Step

* We Were Such a Good and Loving Invention

I ask you: what is the next step?

Have you experienced this before, the person who just disappears, emotionally, from your life? One minute he or she is there, wanting you, with you 100%, your heart seemingly attached to his or hers, and then—what? Pfft. Void. Inoperative. Nullity.

Perhaps this is the Nothing she meant.

What could I do? The pain was crippling.

I wrote letter after letter, then, when they were dying along the way, poem after poem.

This is a fairly typical example:

S Again (Exuviae)

> "The lips extract more from a kiss than they can say."
> Elliot Baker

I inhaled the sheets
after you left.
I imbibed you.

You shrugged off your
skin like a snake,
golden, freckled, aromatic.
You were a snake.

It wasn't even what I felt. S was not a snake. She simply did not love me. My friend, Norm, who is wise in the ways and means of the human heart said this: Forgive her for not loving you.

I couldn't.

*Bobo, the Unmateable Gorilla and Everyone Except Erland Josephson

Norm told me to start dating. Everyone told me to start dating.

That's not true.

Not everyone. Erland Josephson, the great Swedish actor, for instance, did not tell me to start dating.

I wanted to prove people wrong. I wanted to be Bobo, the unmateable gorilla.

I peed in my cage.

I slept in straw.

I woke everyday with my heart scuffed, kicked around the block.

I woke everyday, Sharless, as bad a feeling as Satan taking your soul.

I played "Mr. Pitiful" over and over. Music from the other side of the void.

Kill me.

*Sad Teachers of English Comp

Then I met a woman. In a bar.

I'm not the meet-a-woman-in-a-bar kind of guy. You have to believe me. I'm not even a bar kind of guy.

But Norm and I, occasionally, went to a sad little watering hole called The Beer Garden of your Dreams. A stupid name and a relatively stupid place, except that what passed for the literati in Oklahoma City drank there. Sad teachers of English Comp who have a novel in their drawers and a poem ready on their lips. Who meet other teachers of English Comp weekend nights, to trade quips and barbs and Lakeside Poets quotes.

Also local actors and actresses. But, normally, that was Thursday nights. What was referred to as Thespian Thursdays, when the place would fill with the din of the overly vivacious, the overly affected. The overly dramatic, the overly playful. Get it? The fuliginous atmosphere would be thick with air kisses, small things like gnats, and just as annoying.

But Norm and I found it as good a place as any to act out our sad bastards routine. Except that Norm wasn't as sad as he used to be, which rankled a bit, though I was happy for him. Norm had just connected with Donna, an old high school friend of ours who recently divorced. Norm and Donna were inseparable, which occasionally made me feel left out, but also occasionally made me very happy for the both of them.

But Donna was visiting her grandmother in Wichita Falls and Norm and I had the evening to ourselves. It almost felt like old times.

"*The Prisoner*, now there was a great TV series," Norm had just said.

I was nodding in ready agreement when I saw her. She was wearing a white dress that stood out in the murk like the glow of fairies in a dolmen. She was talking animatedly with an older woman (I later found out it was her mother)—and she was stunningly beautiful. So beautiful that I had no chance with her. So beautiful that I figured what the fuck. Why not get shot down by the preeminent?

"Excuse me," I said to Norm's dumbfounded face.

I rose and walked toward her as if I were walking my last mile.

She grew closer—a wafting spirit.

I stood next to her chair and waited for her to finish what she was saying. She looked up at me the way the centurion looked up at Jesus on the cross.

"You're the most exquisite thing I've ever seen," I said. When you ain't got nuthin, you got nuthin to lose.

Her name was Kim. Well, it probably still is, though she has sunk into that small corner of hell known as People from our Past. They disappear—they really do, you can't find their names in any phone book. Hire a detective—go ahead. It would be foolish on your part. They're as gone as the Hittites.

On our first date I found out that it was the word "exquisite" that did it. She simply had never been called exquisite before.

*At the Earliest Dark Answer

Dating Kim was imprudent, irrational. It was self-destructive.

Sometimes before going to bed with her I would throw up from sheer anticipation.

But, friends, I went to bed with her. She was—how can I describe it—she glowed, like a star. She was soft white light.

Naked, her skin was alabastrine. No, it was alabastrine when clothed, too, but, naked it seemed to come out of a cocoon, like something incipient, something just being born.

Kim.

I managed a few good nights with her. It wasn't easy, what with the nausea and all. But, then again, she was medicinal. And, when we went out, other men would hit on her as if I were invisible. I wanted to be invisible, a cipher.

And I needed to forget Sharilyn, at least for a while. I need to plug back into my own body.

I knew Kim would move on.

Once after a particularly strenuous rut, I looked into her pellucid blue eyes and I saw the only woman I could ever marry. This is what strenuous ruts can do to you, a total derangement of the senses, of sense. Lordy.

Even my best friends didn't know what she was doing with me. I didn't know, surely.

Yet, I have those memories like freshly milled dreams, of Kim naked, of entering Kim, of our hopeless, helpless, glimmering coupling.

*Goodbye, Kim

Jack looked at his watch again. She was now one hour late. Jack knew what this meant. She didn't care. Kim was showing him that she didn't care.

And he knew why. Because he had been precipitant. Because the marriage proposal had come too early, and with too much heat. But she was so beautiful—she could knock you down with her smile—he was trying to secure her. Instead she ran. This was conventional human behavior.

After another half hour Jack left his house. He left his house so that when she did show up—if she did show up—he would not be there. Instead he walked up into the cove and sat on the curb, looking down at his own house, a small yellow luminescence in the darkness. It was late at night.

Jack had been sitting there fifteen minutes when Kim arrived. She pulled up to the curb, as opposed to pulling into the driveway the way she used to. He tried not to read anything into that.

She stood underneath his porch light, knocking on the door. Her knocking was not very convincing. Kim stepped back, scanned the neighborhood. Her face was as calm as the breast of a lake.

Jack hated her at that moment. His hate burned in him like the crashing of stars. Jack was all alone in the world, his love washing away in the insouciant gaze of his erstwhile lover. Still, she was so damned beautiful. O how his heart sang!

***Goodbye, Kim Part Two**

It didn't hurt too badly when Kim left. I rushed her like I was drowning and she was my only hope. Jesus, how embarrassing. Did I really ask her to marry me? I did. Did I mean it? In retrospect, of course not—what a disaster that would have been. At the time? Oh, yeah, I meant it. I meant it in spades. I mean, what the fuck.

In "Hinged to Forgetfulness like a Door" Richard Brautigan says, "too many times she slept like/a mechanical deer in my caresses,/and I ached in the metal silence/of her dreams."

Kim, my mechanical deer. Goodbye.

*Back to the Way I Was Before

Back to the way I was before Kim, I started moping around at work, making everyone either (1) feel sorry for me, or (2) wish that I would dry up and blow away. I was a sickly apparition.

What happened to the good feeling Kim engendered, the shudder that sexual exhilaration brings and leaves draped over one's soul, like an electric blanket?

I don't know. I felt better about myself, probably. But I wanted to be a sad bastard. It was a persona that Norm and I had perfected but now I played the part alone, like those one-man shows based on a great person's life, Clarence Darrow or Emily Dickinson or Will Rogers.

*I Was in a One Man Show Based on Bob Denver

I felt like I was stuck in a one-man show based on someone inconsequential, Bob Denver, or John Denver, or Denver Pyle. You get the idea.

I was walking around, bumping into people.

My friend, Eddie, thinks this is how two people meet, how you'll eventually meet your mate, walking around bumping into people.

I've lost touch with Eddie. This is what happens in middle-age, the friends you lose you don't regain, you don't find replacements for.

I bumped into many people. I had some one-night stands, with women whose names I don't even remember. This is awful.

I think this is awful.

Richard Brautigan said something like "if I was a turd I wouldn't attract a female fly." That was how it was most nights, nights when I wasn't pounding myself against a stranger with acne on her shoulders, or a slight droop to one eye.

That's not fair. That's ugly.

I bedded some agreeable women. I just don't remember them.

I'm not worth spit.

*Too Many Lifetimes Like This One, Right?

Around this time I heard that Richard Brautigan died. Which means it would be 1984, Orwell's year.

Which means I had been bumping into people for too long.

I mourned the loss of Richard Brautigan the way I had mourned the untimely death of John Lennon, killed on a New York sidewalk, 8 years earlier, by a miserable, moon-stricken soldier with a toy called a handgun and a dog-eared copy of *Catcher in the Rye*. At least he was not carrying *The Pill Versus The Springhill Mine Disaster*.

Then what happened—why you are listening to this tale—would never have happened. Probably. It would have been the kind of sign I don't believe in but heed nevertheless. Are you like that?

I wrote this about John Lennon:

The Day John Lennon Died

The day John Lennon died
it did not rain blood.
The birds did not come
unstuck from the sky.

The day John Lennon died
no one gave birth to
a monster. No one wept acid.
It was just an ordinary day.

The day John Lennon died
was an ordinary day with an
ordinary stranger, a simple greeting
and a malignant, magical gun.

When I heard about Richard Brautigan's death I didn't write a poem. I cried. I cried as if he were my father. My own father was still alive—is still alive!—living in Oklahoma City, retired from working for Big Oil.

***The Story of His Death**

So the Wind Won't Blow it All Away, ironically, or maybe not so, when you think about its whimsical author, was published in 1982. Two years later Richard Brautigan shot himself to death in his second home in Bolinas, California. The body was not found until many weeks later, on October 25, 1984.

Why so long to find the body? Had he alienated his many friends to the point where they rarely called, rarely dropped in?

The story I heard was that he ran into, on the streets of San Francisco, his Japanese ex-wife, Aki, who had spurned him years earlier, unexpectedly, and he was stricken as if Death Itself, with full Cerement and Sickle, grinned at him. And perhaps it had. Perhaps that's the way he felt.

The story I heard was that he rushed home—like Hemingway he couldn't wait to get that gun into his fervent hands—and blew his face away. When they found him the body had been eaten by the things that eat bodies. They ID'd him by his clothing.

Some said it was the hooch, too.

They held a wake for "the poet of the hippie era" on Halloween. This is appropriate somehow. (See "Trick or Treating Down to the Sea in Ships," in *Revenge of the Lawn*) And it explains a lot, about pretend hauntings, about real hauntings, about the ghosts of those we worship and how they can enter our lives as easily as death sneaks in the back door you were sure you locked.

In "The Final Ride," R. B. wrote, "The act of dying is like hitchhiking into a strange town, late at night, where it is cold and raining, and you are alone again."

*Alone Again

I was more alone. I was Sharless, Kimless, Richardless. Hopeless.

I was as sad as the eyeball of sorrow behind a shroud. Shattered like stormy spray.

I needed a shot of a tired god.

Norm called.

I told him my name was Noman.

Eddie called.

I answered the phone with a recording of whales, beached and dying, squonking into the distant seas, about their sad and misguided lives.

My mother called.

I told her I had murdered sleep.

She told my sister to call.

I told my sister, Joy, I'd just gotten back from Heartbreak and I was on my way to Desuetude.

Vita (an old flame become friend, henceforward called Lovely Vita Meter Maid) phoned.

I told Vita that I had died between her thighs and they forgot to resuscitate me.

Norm called back.

I told him he was horsing a deadbeat.

I was living on hotdogs from the microwave and milk.

The milk wasn't always fresh.

I was alone again.

My Brother, Lark, called. It was only to tell me a joke. Lark had jokes the way most men had (have) gas, or herpes.

I don't remember the joke.

The world had (has) possibilities. I was soon to discover how the world has possibilities when you are tethered to the loose end of a runaway rocket. How the world shakes its dusty blanket and out come fireflies and Solomon's Seal.

Just when it is darkest the universe reminds you that it has a little magic left.

Friends.

I saw a ghost.

*A Study in Oklahoma City Flowers

I went to the Botanical Gardens. I don't know why I did. I don't know an aster from a rhododendron. I don't know a monkshood from a hellebore. I don't know a...you get it.

I wandered the varicolored paths, lost in my zoomy head. I was still an exercise in self-pity but something else had entered in. A chill. A calm, as if I were at sea and the storm had passed.

I was almost smiling as I walked. I was beyond love, beyond the search for the Elusive Feminine.

I stopped next to a bloom with a rather priapic, show-offy countenance. I said, "How came you to be, thou Phallic Flower?"

I didn't really say that but let's say I did for the sake of the story.

I bent closer to the flower and my background went blurry as my foreground grew sharp and distinct. The flower smiled back.

In the backdrop blur I noticed, became aware of gradually, a figure in a beat-up chapeau, black pants faded to grey, a patchwork vest, a Western hat of indeterminate shape, tossed onto a head of chin-length blond hair. Or so it seemed in the miasma of my periphery.

I stood up. I refocused on the background and the herbarium took shape. The figure in the hat in front of it did not. It remained—and you're way ahead of me I know—blurry, wavery, indistinct.

But the watery vision—this shabby apparition—looked like Richard Brautigan.

And, of course, it was.

Returned to the planet as pure spirit, manifesting itself in Oklahoma City, before an obscure, loveless bookstore clerk and bad poet.

Why? you want to ask. Go ahead. Ask why. I did. Do.

Why me?

It's the eternal question—we all must decide "I am" and then decide what we are going to do with "being." Mustn't we?

We all ask, Why me.

***Why Me?**

I slowly raised my hand. The figure slowly raised his. Was it a mirror, a circus mirror, reflecting only my cloudcuckooland condition?

I walked toward him and as I did he became more corporeal. Not entirely flesh and bone but more distinct. And I recognized him.

I almost wept.

The poet of my imagination had come to rescue me from my imagination. That was my first thought. He had been summoned, like Clarence in *It's a Wonderful Life*.

I suppose I felt in need of Heavenly Intervention.

Where there is need there is deliverance? No. I did not, do not, believe that.

Yet, here I was, face to face with a man for whom I had once concocted a Holy Search.

"Hello, Mr. Brautigan," I said, just as if I were greeting a customer in the bookstore, the brother of the owner, say, or the mayor's secretary.

"You have the better of me," he said. His voice was higher than I thought it would be. I expected a bass-baritone, a cowboy voice.

It was more child-like, sweeter.

But, he did not know me. There went my theory on why he was here.

"Jack," I said and I shot out a hand.

He grasped my hand. It was like shaking hands with mist.

I looked at my palm.

"I'm a phantom," he said, like an apology.

"I didn't mean to embarrass you," I said.

"Nah," he answered.

We both stood there, amid nature's plenipotence.

"Where am I?" Richard Brautigan's ghost asked me.

FOUR: Following Richard Brautigan

*The Galileo Hitchhiker

The afternoon of my first sighting was a numinous time, a liminal experience. If I was to be haunted I was going to be the best gull that ever by spirits was visited. I was going to outScrooge Scrooge.

Now, in retrospect, and readers you have that advantage that I did not at the time, the advantage of hindsight, I see that I was trying to fill gaps. I was ripe for a new kind of quest, similar to my initial quest, the one that ended up with my sortilege at the hands of the witchy Sharilyn, save this quest involved the paranormal. Now, you of little faith, you who do not believe in what you cannot tape to the refrigerator, stand aside. From hereon out we will be in a place of otherness. I wanted to be haunted, see, I needed it, because I was bereft, of love, of spirituality, of a goddamn raison d'etre.

I needed my ghost the way man needs love and food and sex, the way Columbus needed to be the discoverer of Something, he didn't care what. The way Galileo needed the heavens to root around in. The way DaVinci needed wings.

This begins the section known as Following Richard Brautigan.

Thus it begins.

*As the Bruises Fade, the Lightning Aches

The next day, at the bookstore, Lovely Vita Meter Maid showed up, unannounced, unanticipated.

She looked like the lamb that sitteth meke and stille, as leef on lynde.

She looked like an angel.

She was wearing a shirt with straps—I don't know how to talk about women's clothing. It was a shirt with straps. There was warm skin in the air.

There were shoulders, wide like riverbanks, lentiginous, as if sprinkled with flour. Flowers. There was a formidable forehead, with a sweet sheen of dew. There was a slightly turned up nose, brown hair almost blond, and lips like sleeping roses.

There were tears in the corners of each eye, tiny diamonds.

"What is it?" I asked because I am a man with feelings.

"I think my husband is leaving me."

"Mark?"

She looked at me as if I were in sixth grade and had just made a smartass reply to the teacher's earnest query.

"Sorry," I said. "What do you mean 'think'?"

"Well, he left this morning without kissing me."

"Lovely Vita—" I began.

"Not just that, stupidhead. He said he was feeling restless."

"Restless."

"As in having an affair."

"You're reading that into it."

"Maybe."

"Well, then."

"I know. But he didn't kiss me."

"And he always does, every morning, without fail."

"Yes."

What must that be like? That there are such people in the world. "Wait before panicking dear," I said, putting my hand on her freckled and fresh shoulder.

"You're right. I may be getting my period."

I had been around enough women to accept this awkward segue with grace.

"Thanks, Jack," LVMM now said. And she kissed me on the cheek.

I fully expected, when I got home, that there would be a set of lips branded on my face, like a birthmark. A rebirth mark. It had been a long time since Lovely Vita Meter Maid had ever set her mouth upon me. Something lived, some theurgy. I almost forgot my ghost.

*I Was Trying To Describe You to Someone

When I got home that night—it had been a day of no small energy expenditure, new books coming in like an armada docking, a surly owner, a nasty customer—I began to wonder how I could contact Richard Brautigan's phantom again. I had to assume he would contact me.

Otherwise this story would involve an improbable medium, some spirit knocking, and a séance with a couple of tourists from Gold Hill, Oregon. A woman with a swami turban, a phony gypsy accent, glass beads that tinkled at the approach of the lares and penates. Knockknock jokes. Forget it.

Richard was waiting for me in my bedroom. He was sitting on the edge of my bed, his mustache drooping with perplexity. I can't describe him. He didn't glow like sulphur or waft about like a wind-blown scarf. He just sat there, sad, frozen, a befuddled poltergeist.

"Hello Jack," he said.

"Richard," I tried.

"Please call me Richard," he said. He hadn't looked up yet.

"Richard," I repeated. Was this ghost aphasia or just Richard's loopiness?

He looked up now, his face long and lassitudinous, like a shower-beaten bloom.

"Ah, Jack."

"You look sad," I said. I have a penchant for stating the obvious. Sometimes you can get by doing this. Try it.

"I'm not so much sad," he said, now turning his weathered face to me, a gentle face that needed ironing. "I'm sunk in wonder."

"That doesn't sound so bad."

"No, no. It's not," Richard Brautigan's ghost said.

"Ok."

Now he smiled. It was the smile that Merlin smiled for Wart.

"It's not so bad, is it?" He put his large hands on his knees as if preparing to rise.

He did not rise, immediately.

"Wanna go someplace?" he said.

***It Begins as a Stroll and with a Rainbow**

Hence began the peripatetic part of my life with Richard Brautigan's afterdeath self. We began, simply enough, with a walk around my neighborhood. I think he just wanted to get out into the air, sort of test his new state of being. One step at a time.

When we passed my neighbor, Mrs. Glockomorra's house, she had the lawn sprinkler going. She always had the lawn sprinkler going. It defined Mrs. Glockomorra.

But, on this evening, the setting sun was throwing a rainbow into the mist. Richard stopped dead—forgive me—in his tracks and stared at the Roygbiv, as if it were the most astonishing magic trick he had ever seen.

"What is it?" I asked.

"Beautiful," he said.

"The—"

"It's still beautiful," he said.

And I understood. At least partly.

Mrs. Glockomorra came out onto her porch and looked at us suspiciously.

"Good day, Mrs. Glockomorra," I shouted. She was, is, partly deaf.

"Beautiful," Richard shouted.

Mrs. Glockomorra gathered her omnipresent bathrobe about her—as if Richard were intent on violation—and disappeared into her house.

Richard looked at me and I think his eyes were asking me if he had done something wrong.

I smiled reassurance.

*On My Thirtieth Birthday One of the Twins Had Freckles

It was around this time that I celebrated my thirtieth birthday.

I took the day off from the bookstore—I don't know what I expected. "Mrs. Tweedy," I fairly bawled into the phone, "I'm thirty today and I'm calling in well." Thankfully, she laughed. I had no plans and no plans to have plans. I think I thought I would spend the day with my spirit pal, that we would do the things that best friends do. After the day we took a walk around the block, talking of inconsequentials, what books I liked, whose prose style was stilted, whether I preferred Charlie Chaplin over Buster Keaton, I thought Richard and I were going to be spending all our spare time together. Did a haint have other appointments? Did they haunt two people simultaneously? Where is he when not haunting me? is a reasonable query.

I didn't—don't—know. But I thought—it's my 30th birthday—something remarkable could happen.

And that evening, sunk into self-pity like a For Sale sign on my childhood home, I lay nearly comatose in front of some inane sitcom, having skipped dinner—surely someone would bring me food!—and feeling friendless and unfriendly.

Then the phone rang.

It was Norm. He asked if I was going to be home for a while. I allowed as to how I was. Ok, he said, and hung up.

A surprise, I surmised.

And about an hour later there was a knock on the door and standing on my front porch, under the buggy, yellow light, was Norm and two identical skinny girls, pretty girls, with implausible pigtails and faces like faith's final hue.

"Good," Norm said, and ushered the girls inside. They, I think you could call it, giggled.

"Happy birthday, buddy," Norm said, his smile like a slice in an apple.

"Thanks," I said.

"Vicki and Valerie," Norm said.

"Hello," I said.

"Ok," Norm said. "I'll leave you then."

"Wha—" I said, and Norm put a single digit to his lips, the universal sign for shut-up.

He left and I looked at the girls. They were maybe 20 years old, if that, thin as groat, and the only difference between them was that one of them had about 15 freckles on her turned up nose. They wore very short skirts and very short shirts, which revealed identical belly buttons, with identical rose vine tattoos ringing them.

"Norm said it's your like 30th birthday and that you could have us for it," one of them said. The other smiled a vixen smile, above which freckles danced.

"Good lord," I said.

It would have been quite a night. A threesome is embarrassing unless you've just turned thirty and you think you deserve it all. I thought I deserved it all. Except I was so far from turned on by their admittedly lovely presence that sex may as well have been a trip to Xanadu. Or a ride into the tunnel of love on the river Styx. I was asexual. I was a one-celled organism.

The twins giggled and tootled and whispered to each other. I invited them to sit with me and watch *Notorious* which I had rented as my birthday movie. They sat on either side of me, sure, I am guessing, that I would soon be on them like the grateful animal Norm had outlined. When the movie was over we all three stood and I bussed each of them gently on their fresh cheeks.

"Goodbye," I said. "Thanks for the birthday visit."

They looked at me the way Ingrid Bergman looked at that spiked glass of milk.

The next day I called Norm and thanked him for the best birthday present I'd ever gotten. I didn't ask if I could ever see the twins again. I knew I couldn't. Nor did I merit another visit. Few men do.

*Lark Called with a Joke (1)

The Lone Ranger is captured by savages. The chief is about to put the Lone Ranger to death but grants him three wishes and three night's stay. The first wish the Lone Ranger chooses is to talk to his horse, Trigger. He whispers in Trigger's ear and Trigger gallops away. A few hours later he returns with a beautiful brunette. The chief smiles and leaves the Lone Ranger and the woman alone. The next morning the chief again asks The Lone Ranger for his wish and again he asks to speak to his horse. He whispers in Trigger's ear and off gallops the horse. Trigger returns a few hours later with a beautiful blond. The chief smiles and again leaves The Lone Ranger with his woman. The next morning the chief says, "That is a remarkable horse you have there. But, before I put you to death, you have one more wish." The Lone Ranger again asks for his horse. Trigger is brought in and The Lone Ranger approaches him and grabs him around the neck. He whispers in his ear, through grit teeth, "Now, listen to me very closely. I want you to bring me a *posse*."

*Another Lifetime

I worked on at the bookstore, an indentured servant, a gypsy moth with its wings clipped. Yet, I was vaguely happy. Days at work, nights writing. I was writing again. This was a good thing.

And on the seventh day Richard Brautigan's ghost appeared again.

I was working in the science fiction section, putting brilliant, bright, colorful paperbacks into a wire rack, Doc Savage novels, Edgar Rice Burroughs, Bradbury, Arthur C. Clarke, Lem, Heinlein, an inordinate number of E. E. "Doc" Smith novels, something called the Gor Series. I've often said, that if I had another lifetime I'd read more genre fiction. It seems a crime sometimes to get enmeshed in some otherworld fantasy, with aliens and talking animal creatures, etc. when there are novels by Dostoyevsky that I've yet to get to. Tolstoy, Virginia Woolf. This is elitism, yes, but there it is. I have read *Fahrenheit 451*. And *Childhood's End*. Maybe one or two more. And I enjoyed them.

Richard was suddenly there, looking over my shoulder.

He smiled when I turned.

"What are those?" he asked.

"Science fiction novels."

"Hm."

"You ever read any?"

"Hm?"

"Science fiction. You ever read any?"

"I think so," Richard said, and he put a hand in his mustache.

"I've—"

"Conan the Barbarian!"

"Ah," I said.

"That was a good book."

"Ok. I haven't read it. I've read some Bradbury."

"I've read some Bradbury."

"Have—"

"Do you like to fish?" Richard Brautigan's ghost asked me.

This was a question I was dreading.

"I don't actually," I said, gently.

"Huh." He thought this over for a minute.

"No fishing then."

"Sorry."

"Not at all. You wanna go for a coffee?"

"I get off in an hour," I said.

"I'll wait outside."

But when I got off work—it was probably more like an hour and a half—he wasn't there. I began to think that perhaps he couldn't control his comings and goings.

And furthermore, he was perhaps flummoxed as to the subject of his current assignment. I think he may have been slightly disappointed in me.

***We Pledge Ourselves to Randomness**

But the next morning, my day off, there he was in the kitchen, when I stumbled in, one leg still numb from sleep, badly in need of coffee.

Richard already had a pot going and he was quietly sipping from a cup of black. Leaning against the sink like some casual daemon.

"Good morning," I said, trying to invest my voice with insouciance, as if I were getting used to a specter appearing at odd times, whenever and wherever.

"Paper's not here yet," he said.

"I don't take the paper," I said.

"Ok," he said, sipping his hot joe. He seemed sad.

"Everything ok?" I asked, taking my cup and sitting with him at my crappy little aluminum kitchen table.

"Sure," he said. It was the most melancholy "sure" I'd ever

heard.

"What is it?" I asked, the coffee starting its necessary jangle in me.

"Oklahoma City," he said. "Why am I in Oklahoma City?'

"I don't know, I'm sure."

"I could just as easily be in Ames, Iowa, or Scranton, Pennsylvania. Or Lima, Peru."

"I suppose so."

"It's random."

"So much is."

Now he turned his face toward me.

"You're right. So much is. That's just it. That's the crux of it, what I've been trying to get at. Let randomness be our merry-go-round. Let it be our flashlight. Let randomness be our planisphere."

"Ok," I said.

I had no idea what he was talking about.

Then something clicked in me.

"Richard, have you been sent here? Am I—what?—an objective?"

"No," he said.

"Where were you, I mean, right before you appeared to me in the Botanic Gardens?" I don't know why I hadn't asked this before. It seemed crucial to our relationship—if this is a relationship.

Richard Brautigan's ghost smiled a smile a big cat might enjoy.

"Hell, son," he said. "I can't talk about that."

And that was that. That was where we stood. How we were to continue.

"Whatchoo wanna do today," he asked.

"I'm yours," I said.

"Right," Richard Brautigan's ghost said.

*The Mausoleum Telephone

While I was showering, the phone rang. Richard let it ring. It rang like a bell inside a mausoleum.

I finally grabbed it on the tenth ring. I was dripping in my hallway.

"Jack, you busy?" a tear-stained voice said.

It was Lovely Vita Meter Maid.

"In the shower," I said. "What's wrong?"

"He—" she said. There was a snuffly sound like corduroy on a microphone.

"He left you," I finished.

"Y-es," she said.

"Bastard."

"Jack—"

"We'll be right over," I said. Only after I hung up did I realize the problematic scenario I had just suggested. Where did that "we" come from?

*Wrapping Ourselves in Cocoons of Desire and Need and Fleshly Love

Richard and I arrived at Vita's, stoked on caffeine, and only apparently otherworldly. It honestly didn't occur to me until we were in my Toyota and on the way there that I had to admit to another flesh and blood human being that I had been communing with the spirit world.

On the drive over I looked at Richard, sitting there in his

ubiquitous slouch hat and dusty clothing. He looked like something taken out of the attic of the 60s, slightly musty, slightly off-center, but ripe with nostalgic *frisson*.

Richard caught my glances and looked at me with his sad eyes. He smiled that smile of his, the one I keep mentioning, the one that says, life, friends is boring…

"This is your woman?" Richard asked when we got out of the car.

"No, no," I assured him. "We're exes, but Vita is married—that is, she has been married, perhaps up until today. She and her husband are having…"

The opening of the door interrupted my explanation. LVMM rushed into my arms. She was weeping like a tired child.

I held her sobbing body and it felt good to me.

It brought back the past like the sting of a tattooist's needle.

I remembered the times Vita and I had cohered, met like humans and turned into fiery angels, in the manacles of the bedclothes, wrapping ourselves in cocoons of desire and need and fleshly love. I suddenly flashed on her lovely body, its boyish shoulders, its small breasts and motherly hips and thighs as perfect as an astronomical chart.

All this in the flash of her holding me.

But the immediate need was for succor, for comfort, for a little bit of what friendship carries in its back pocket.

"Sweet," I said, "It's gonna be ok." How could I know?

"O Jack," she said, and her snotty nose and bubbly mouth were against my neck, nudging my shirt collar aside.

"Tell me what happened."

"I-I-I-…"

"Take your time, I'm here," I said, stroking her back and shoulders.

She gulped, she gasped. She snuffled some more into my neck.

I was tingling but trying not to.

"He-he-he," she said.

She was not laughing. Nothing was funny.

"He left?"

"Y-yes."

"Listen, sweet, that's good. In the long run, that's good. You were unhappy."

"Shit."

"Ok."

"I'm, just, I'm unlovable."

"Dearheart, you're about the most loveable female on the planet."

Here she pulled back and looked me in the eye.

Her eyes were, are, blue like fairy-flax.

"You've always been the sweetest man," she said.

The sweetest man. Like a cousin. A brother. A Friend.

Hang on, Jack.

"You know I love you," I said.

"Yes, I do."

"Ok."

"You always have."

Well, this was partly true. I certainly wasn't going to argue.

"And I'm always here—right? You see, you call Jack and Jack comes."

"Yes."

"You love Jack."

I didn't, don't, know what I was doing.

Again the eyes.

"I do," she said, after a pause so pregnant I thought I was going to have to deliver.

"You'll get through this. I'll help you. If he's left for good—and, to be honest, I hope he has—we'll make plans. Ok?"

"You don't like Mark?"

"No. I don't like Mark. I've never liked Mark. I always thought you opted down."

"Opted down."

"You know what I mean."

"Yes."

"Mark has never been good to you, nor good enough for you."

Lovely Vita Meter Maid thought this over.

"You're right."

"I am."

"Jack. Kiss me, Jack."

And reader I did. Of course, I did.

***Oh, Shit.**

"Oh, shit," I said. "Vita, darling, this is, um, Richard."

I swung my arm out as if I were presenting not only my ghostly companion but my car and the whole western end of her neighborhood.

There was no one there.

I blinked a few times. The car's passenger side door stood open.

"He was right here," I said, stupidly.

"Who?" Vita asked, blinking away more tears.

"My friend, uh, Richard."

"I don't know Richard. You mean Richard Neighbors, from high school?"

"No, no."

"Richard who?"

"Never mind," I said.

I looked at her.

"You ok now? I can leave. I can leave and your tears will dry up and we shall resume our lives until you need me again and we will work on rectifying this situation…"

I was babbling. Rectifying—Jesus.

"Sure. I'm ok."

"Convince me."

Here she kissed me again, deeper, her tongue a silkie in the seawater of my hungry mouth. Fah. That's some badly overheated prose. Stick with me.

"That's convincing?" I said. I didn't mean to make it a question.

"I'm ok," she said and skipped back inside.

I stood on the front lawn of LVMM's home—the home she had fabricated with her shitheel husband of 3 years, a slight erection in my pants, my head full of tangled emotions, like the flight of dark shadows just before dawn.

My head a place where haints lived.

***She Kissed Me vs. What Men Have Learned**

"She kissed you?"

"Yes."

"Lovely Vita Meter Maid?"

"Norm, that's what I'm telling you."

"This is fantastic."

"It isn't."

"No, no, it is. You guys are unfinished business. You should have stayed together."

"Remind me why we didn't."

"I don't know. She said something about she didn't deserve you, that you loved hard and well and she didn't know how. That she was not going to make you happy."

"All lies. All deflection."

"Of course."

"We've learned since how to read those runes."

"We have."

"We're better men for it."

"If you say so."

"You're supposed to be bolstering me here."

"Right."

"It's good?"

"Yes. She kissed you. This is one of the four most beautiful women that God has made. She is the Sun. She is the reason God doesn't just flood the whole damn world again."

"Norm."

"Ok. Look, take it slow. Maybe there's happiness there. Maybe not. Is it any different from any other relationship?"

"It's not a relationship. Our Lovely Vita Meter Maid is married. Mark."

"Shitheel."

"Still."

"For now, I should try not to think about it, right? This is your counsel. The timing is a little agley."

"If you say so."

"I do. I think I do."

"Ok."

"She kissed me."

"I know."

***Oklahoma Is a Garden of Eden**

Richard Brautigan's ghost disappeared for a while. Ghosts disappear; it's part of their MO.

So, my life settled back into its drab SSDD, selling the odd Updike novel in amongst the scores of romance crapola. Ah, those customers—the Updikean ones—are light unto my path. This was a young college student—his face a pebbly acne field, under a clown's mop of orange hair. I liked him immediately. He smiled a shy smile when he entered and made a beeline for Fiction, which endeared him to me.

And when he bought *A Month of Sundays*, my heart zinged. I gave him a heartier than usual "thanks" and I thought some transmission passed between us. Something human and real.

Of such moments my days are made.

And, I think it was a Thursday night, my late night, when a young woman, wearing a midriff top and low-slung jeans, came in, marched up to the front counter, where I lurked like Count Alucard, and spoke these words:

"Have you heard of a book called *Please Plant this Book*?"

Her eyes were black. Her makeup heavy. And her midriff flat like polished brass. I suddenly remembered the twins, whose midriff tops promised further flesh.

"Yes," I began. Where to go with this?

"Yes," I said again. "Um, Richard Brautigan. It's out of print, of course, near impossible to find. You know, when I was out in San Francisco, I was kind of on a holy quest to find Mr. Brautigan, and I frequented City Lights bookstore, which is really Mecca for pilgrims such as I, among other bookstores, both dusty and bright, and though I was sidetracked by a siren named Sharilyn, who took me to her bed and turned me inside out, and almost made me forget that I had come to the city to find the heart of Richard Brautigan, I did indeed make the rounds of literary stops and nowhere, nowhere, dear heart, did I find a copy of *Please Plant this Book*. With or without its seed packets. It is that thing upon which quests are initiated. It is as rare as hedgerows in the wild."

I think I said all this.

If I did, it was part loopy, part prevarication. I did indeed lay eyes on a copy of said Holy Book. Didn't I? Flip back.

Well. It went something like that. And the poor girl, who only wanted to ask for a book of poems, was momentarily skimble-skambled.

She regathered herself and spoke again, her eye on me like a glint off a sword.

"So. No way to get it. Am I getting the gist?"

"Jack," I said, and put out my hand.

A smile slipped onto her mouth like a kiss.

"Helen," she said.

"Of Troy?" I countered, from behind the counter.

"You're funny, mister."

I thought the 'mister' was a roadblock, an indicator from her that she was a child and I was a graybeard.

But, friends, she then said this:

"278-7484."

"Ah," I said, and here I too inserted a smile.

"How about tonight?" I asked.

And Helen came into my life.

***Her Name Was (is) Helen Holland**

Only later did I appreciate that Helen came to me via Richard Brautigan. Perhaps this is the quest, the point of, the reason I undertook it.

On our first date—we saw a Robert Altman movie, I think, my memory fuzzes this part—and went back to her shoddy apartment, where she stood in the doorway like Ozymandias, blocking one possible ending to the story.

But she did offer up her rosebud mouth, which was wet and warm and flowing with juices like a plum.

I wanted nothing more than to kiss Helen again. And again. I went home that first night and dreamt about her, and in every manifestation, she was Womanhood, moist and ready.

Helen was 19 years old, a sophomore at Oklahoma City University.

And I was older.

Yet smitten, foolish under her youthful spell.

When we came together—I believe it was date three—she moved under me and on top of me like God's immaculate machine. She was lovely, sweet and smooth and I relished making love with her. She was dewy and fresh and tasted good to me.

I forgot many things in those Days of Helen.

I forgot my friend, Lovely Vita Meter Maid, and her marital woes.

I forgot Norm and his wild and affable ways, a friend as solid as a pit in a peach. And Norm's new love, his Ma-donna, about whom he was gentlemanly mute.

I forgot and forgot until I was alive only to Helen's mouth and Helen's hands.

I forgot that I was haunted.

***The Short Term Series of Why Why Why**

Life is a series of hellos and goodbyes. Someone said that.

My life has certainly been that, a series, like one that gets cancelled into its second season.

Helen—even though I knew she was just a stop on my way to either Heaven or Gehenna—was a light, an incandescence, a soft spot in my hard life. Sometimes, when we know things are temporary their innate sweetness is more pronounced, like life itself. Like life itself.

Except I had seen what was after life. Wandering incoherence, a variety of melancholy, and still the eternal questions. Always why why why why.

Helen Holland—here I write your full name so that you know I remember, so that you are not just a signpost, a stopgap, another ghost—I almost loved you. I loved you in every way I was capable at that time. I still see your smile—a hyphen offset my parenthetical dimples.

And I hear your voice, a cartoon character's, with a backbeat of sexy huskiness. It is the huskiness I remember from our time in bed.

Did we do more than go to bed?

We did. We saw some movies. We built a bookcase one day. We went to the Botanical Gardens. I think we went to the Botanical Gardens.

I will talk a little bit more about Helen Holland.

Because I want to. Because she was, is important to me.

Jesus, I think it was Billy Joel who said that.

***A Poem Left Behind**

One night I wrote a poem for Helen and gave it to her on our way to the movies.

Wait.

I wrote the poem the week before. I gave it to Helen on our way to the movies one night.

Better.

It was a love poem, sort of. A romantic poem. An ode.

It went something like this:

I loved you
when you were
a white child.
Fey, like
a sprite,
in my bed
you were
powder, sweet
and plush.

Your skin was
like fresh
fruit. Your body
was a peri's, yet
ripe and erotogenic.
I loved
you and
that's such a
rotten way
to begin
a poem.

The particulars were right though the tone was not. The past tense—why did it occur to me in the middle of things? I didn't think about it when I gave the poem to Helen.

Her response was odd. Unresponsive.

She said, "That's nice."

Gee, that's what poets want to hear.

I smiled and kissed her cheek. She folded the poem and kept it in her hand like a pocketbook.

The movie we saw had Gene Hackman in it. I love Gene Hackman. He was, is, in everything.

I liked the movie. Helen was full of criticism.

She said, "They're dumbing down the story. Basically, it's *Pride and Prejudice* in the Bronx. It's *Love's Labour Lost* with Brooklyn accents and a gritty cityscape background. And some of that dialog. They're not writing for me, that's for sure."

I'm not certain what Helen was getting at. I'm not sure she knew. She was being analytical because she thought people should be analytical. I run into this a lot.

She still looked well-favored in the sodium lights of the parking lot, in the flash photography of the streetlights as we drove home. Her face, in profile, was, is, a Madonna's, her cheek pearlescent.

She went on a bit longer about the movie.

I kept my own counsel. She knew I liked it. I'm not getting at anything.

Then the silence of Lethe's Tide surrounded us. The night was grey with highlights along its edges.

"Where's the poem?" I said.

Helen didn't turn, didn't answer.

I wondered if I had spoken aloud.

"I left it in the theater," she said, finally. She turned toward me and her eyes were sorrowful.

I looked at her. Her cheek was, is pearlescent.

"It's ok," I said, because it was. It was not that high-quality a poem, or even apropos.

That night we made love as if we were old time lovers, slowly, with great composure and with great tenderness. I might have said, "I love you" in the quiet afterwards. In the post-coital stillness.

I hope I didn't. But I might have.

*Love's Not the Way To Treat a Friend

Here's where things began to get a little weird.

Helen and I were at the movies again, same theater, different film. I think it was a French Froth, as I called them, much to Helen's chagrin. I don't want to make it sound like our divergence about movies was anything more than a difference of opinion. We laughed a lot. That's a good thing.

Helen Holland and I laughed a lot.

Why didn't we last?

But, after this particular movie, as we flowed out into the lobby with the parting mass, I happened to look at the crowd coming out of the Gene Hackman movie. And there, in the middle of the crowd, half-hidden by faces like petals on a bough, taller than the surrounding throng, slouch hat askew on ragged hanks of hair, was Richard. It was he, as sure as I'm writing this.

Our streams were moving in different directions.

Once outside I looked around for him. But I couldn't see him. Of course, it makes sense that he would not be heading for a car. He traveled by—what?—disappearing and reappearing. Is there a name for that?

I'd have to ask Richard.

Helen didn't understand my sudden depression, my quick as a no-look pass drop into introspection.

I didn't understand it either.

It was akin to jealousy.

Was Richard Brautigan haunting someone else? Had I done something wrong?

*How To Inflate Your Man with Natter About Mortality

Once in the afterglow of post-coitus, Helen and I lay naked on top of the bedclothes, her finger absently running about in the muck round my limp johnthomas and my sticky curls. She seemed about to say something.

She was about to say something.

"Jack," she began. "You ever think about death?"

This was not strange aftermath confab—it stands to reason. The French, after all, are occasionally spot on.

"Sure," I said.

"You lost anyone close to you?"

"I haven't," I said.

"I lost my mom."

How did I not know this?

"Jesus. I'm sorry. When was this?"

"Long ago. I was 12. Cancer. But fast."

"Sorry."

"No. That's ok. I mean, I wanted to know, you know, what you thought about what happens. After."

I had insider information. I felt like I shouldn't use it. Like I would be answerable to the Universe's Securities and Trade Commission.

"I don't know," I hedged.

"I think there's—something."

"Yeah."

"You don't."

"I do. I most decidedly do."

"Hm."

Helen Holland put her hand around my humid, gummy, pliable manhood, which was for the most part boyhood now. A prepubescent nub.

"You ever seen a ghost?" she asked.

And a weird congruence occurred. My dick began to respond to her encircling, warm palm, and my head spun out of control.

*The Papier-Mâché Trout

"The first trip Richard ever made east, he was standing in Harvard Square, and up Mass. Ave there comes a parade in the very front row of which are four young women. The middle two are carrying a gigantic papier-mâché trout, and the outside two are carrying poles with a banner between them reading, Trout Fishing in America. The parade was for some school in Cambridge named for the book, and Richard's reaction was sheer ecstasy and delight. Once Richard was recognized, he joined the parade. I don't think he had any awareness of how damaging celebrity might be."

Bobbie Louise Hawkins, quoted in *Downstream from Trout Fishing in America*

*Another Sorry Fishing Metaphor

Gradually, I could feel Helen slipping away from me, as if I were standing on a walkway above rapids, holding her by her wet, slippery wrist. I don't understand these things. Helen Holland was a bright, white star of incandescent tenderness and affection, yet, yet, I was moving away from her, in my mind, in my heart.

Can we choose whom we fall in love with?

We cannot.

All we can do is keep fishing, keep bumping into others, keep the doors of the heart open and not bricked up. Men fish with their dicks. Women, I don't know. They are empty bowls, beautiful empty bowls. They are so far advanced as to not be the same species as men.

Most men should be shot.

I should be shot.

But, for now, some more episodes in the soon-to-be-cancelled sitcom (or dramedy, if you will) called My Days with Helen.

Helen and I went to the museum, The Oklahoma City Museum of Art, to see a show of Sargent and Cassatt and Whistler. Helen loved Mary Cassatt, so I did, too. We held hands as we made our slow peregrination around the colorful walls. We must have looked like Hansel and Gretel, on a visit to town, such was our childlike joy with each other and with the art.

Why didn't I love Helen Holland?

Stop.

We're at the museum. We're looking at paintings by geniuses, Master Artisans, pictures that lead you in as if they are dark fairy tales.

In front of one particular Cassatt ("On a Balcony During a Carnival"?) Helen fell in, mesmerized. I craned my neck around, a pandiculation meant only to relax the body, not to distract. And I saw him.

In an adjacent room, standing next to an old woman dressed seemingly for a ball in Hell, complete with a plastic bag full of extra clothing, was Richard Brautigan. He was looking at a piece of modern art—I couldn't see what it was—and he seemed to be as transfixed as Helen by Cassatt.

I tried to get his attention without disturbing my paramour.

I tried this by mental gymnastics and wild facial distortions.

I looked like a maniac, my head turned awkwardly to my right, my face squinching and unsquinching, eyebrows hopping like mad, a crazed Groucho Marx, mouth forming frozen words, words that died before the tongue. I may even have been twitching my nose.

Other museum-goers were looking at me with disgust, distrust, disdain.

Richard was a study in gone.

I didn't know whether to break the two-link chain of affection with Helen and chase madly into the next room. There would follow explanations that I was not prepared to give.

I wasn't ready to introduce the ghost into my workaday life.

Richard moved on, drifting off like smoke. He may have discorporated when he reached the next room—two rooms away—or he may have just vanished in the crowd. I was left standing there, a gommie. My face was tired.

I put a hand to my neck and turned back toward Helen.

She was staring at me.

I smiled.

"You are one strange man," she said.

"Huh," I said.

"What the hell are you looking at?"

*As Lives Die Beside Me I Contemplate My Phantasm

That night, after making love with Helen, after Helen fell asleep, my sperm coagulating inside her sweet body, dying in the admixture of chemicals humans use so as to not produce more humans, I lay awake thinking.

It seemed that Richard was not going to return to my

bedroom—perhaps because it was a place now for concupiscence and estrus—but was he popping in for me at all? He had not acknowledged me in his last two public appearances—yet he was there for me to see, surely. It seemed too much of a coincidence if it was just coincidence.

So, I decided—and this is middle of the night thinking, mind you—that I had to go out alone and hope he materialized. I had to do more things alone. Was this movement away from my dear Helen? Was this what began the break, this otherworldly crack in our twoness?

Or what, what if, Richard would only appear when I was with Helen? This was a curious thought. And if this were the case I could only do one thing.

Introduce Helen Holland to my friend, the revenant.

*Lark Calls with a Joke (2)

These two popes walk into a bar.

*Leo Tolstoy and the Dream-Life Richard

So, where was I?

I was in between.

My real life—represented by the earthy and comely Helen

Holland—was about to collide with what I'd come to call my dream life: Richard.

Was I prepared for that? I thought so. I really did. In hindsight, one can see where one went wrong, map out the esses and stepbacks in your progression. But, at the time, all one sees is what is in front of one. What Tolstoy believed in. What's in front of you.

I took Helen out often. We were a whirlwind of activity such as my life had never known. We went to every art opening, small galleries and large, whether we knew anyone or not. We went to every reading at every school, bookstore or café.

We were a couple, a public couple.

Norm commented on us. Lovely Vita Meter Maid called occasionally, glum and beaten down, asking who this woman was, could she meet her, could she tag along with us, etc. I wasn't giving my old comrade Vita a fair share of my attention, of what she deserved from me.

Forgive me, one and all.

I was trying to trap a ghost, see.

Helen thought I had made a conscious decision that she was now a fixture in my life. She thought our activity meant that she and I were compatible, concrete, in the thick of life and hence, O my friends, in love.

I didn't say one way or another. I loved, love Helen Holland. Just not—oh, hell, you know the old excuse.

Leo Tolstoy, tell me what to do with this white angel in my life—tell me I shouldn't have used her as ghost bait.

"We stopped at perfect days and got out of the car."

***Helen Holland, I Love You**

So, here I was, suddenly a public person, with a mate.

I was a gorilla in a cage.

I did not want other people. I did not want love.

Can that be true? I did not want love?

And did Helen Holland love me? Did she ever say she did? I think so.

I think during sex we both said it. Maybe a couple of times.

Afterwards we avoided each other's eyes.

This is a bad sign.

But, in retrospect, we loved.

I was a gorilla in a cage.

***The Desire To Be Phantasmed**

So out and out we went, here a movie, there a party. Weeks went by and no ghost. I was beginning to sense depression stalking me like a devil unchained, and I felt oddly bereft as if something wonderful had dropped out of my life. The bottom. Yet, at no time, did I think that I had dreamed the whole thing. I felt as sure of my spectre as I did of my girlfriend—perhaps moreso.

Helen and I grew very close during this time. She couldn't know the motivation behind our constant reel of activity but she felt a vital part of my life and, yes, I of hers. I went to places with her friends, a nice bunch, if a little too enthusiastic about their alcohol and their clothes.

Some evenings at home I would find Helen looking at me with, what I think they call, moist eyes. Puppy dog eyes, brimming with emotion. I would answer them with a hard kiss.

My mood grew increasingly dark—I was a pain to be with eventually. I was out of sorts—I wanted my ghost back. I wanted to integrate him and Helen Holland simultaneously into my life. It was time I introduced my lovelife to my, uh, numinous, my supersensual life.

But, my foul mood began to affect Helen—she discerned that something was deeply wrong, and the way humans do, she assumed it had to do with her.

I see it now, in retrospect. The ghost of Richard Brautigan was pushing Helen to the periphery. He was edging her out of my thoughts, out of my heart. Was this the reason we are not together today? I still, at this late date, can't see it clearly enough to answer that.

I only know that I wanted Richard to return. And I would do anything to make it happen.

***God's Atomizer**

It was on a solo trip to the library that Richard returned to me.

I went there to check out a book by Terence Malley, called *Writers for the 70s: Richard Brautigan*. This was the real library, not the library of the imagination, either Borges' or Brautigan's, "the place where losers brought their books."

I was just stooping to a lower shelf to retrieve the paperback

I wanted, jacketed now in a plasticene coat, the way they do with frangible paperbacks in the great and hallowed library systems of the world. I stood up, my eye on the "psychedelicized" photo of Brautigan on the cover.

"He got it wrong," a voice I recognized said, over my shoulder.

I almost hugged the big spirit.

"Hey—" I said.

"He got too much wrong. I mean, I love him, I love the book, but, well, I suppose one doesn't want to be summed up while one is still alive."

"Alive?' I said, without thinking.

Richard looked hurt.

I tried to backpedal.

"Sorry, I—"

"No, no. I was alive when first I read the book," he said, somewhat sadly.

"Whelp. Of course you were. I had this recommended to me by an English professor who knew I was interested in you."

"Interested in me, are you?"

"Well, yes, you know that. Don't you? I mean, I've told you—or have I? I assumed you were haunting me because—"

"Because you were obsessed with me?"

"Not obsessed exactly. I, just—"

"It's ok, Jack. No, I don't know why I'm here with you. Honestly I don't. These things aren't any clearer in the Great Hereafter than they are in your temporal plane."

"Ah," I said. I was a little disappointed. I assumed too much. I thought I was more important than I (was) am.

"So what are we doing? What do you do when you're not with me? Where do you come from and now that you're here, what are you supposed to do?"

"Lead," Richard Brautigan said, and his face squinched up like one of those little rubber masks.

"Lead?" I said back.

"I think so," he said.

"By example?"

"Good God, no," he said.

"Well, I'm easily led, so…"

"Right."

"Where to today?'

"Not today," he said. "I've got a headache."

"You get headaches in the afterlife?" I asked, and it was to be my last question for the day. Richard Brautigan evanesced right in front of me.

I was left alone in the stacks, surrounded by the faintly musty tang of authors dead and living, and a slight mist, as if I had been sprayed by God's atomizer.

*My Name Depends on You

So, now, and for large parts of this tale, the ghost comes and goes. Flitting in and out of my life. Peripatetic and inconstant. Chameleonic. Perhaps this is the nature of incorporeal beings.

Occasionally we had conversations, long into the night, nights when I was away from Helen, nights when I would see Richard's ghost, wavering at the edge of my vision, right before I got off work. I'd see him, partly materialized next to the dumpster in the parking lot as I was getting into my car, and I would go to him, and I would follow him to a bar, and we would sit together and talk.

Where was Helen? What was she thinking?

It never occurred to me.

You're ahead of me—you can see the signposts.

Friends, these talks changed my life. Not that anything earth-shattering was said or discussed. It was just that the numinous presence across from me, the silvery cowboy-hippie-saint-poet, sitting across from me drinking Falstaff, was spirit, pure spirit, and we poor snotty humans, if we can't learn from spirits, we are hopeless. We are gone, a study in gone.

We are nameless.

My name depends on you.

*And Then Cary Granted

One evening Richard and I started talking movies. His knowledge of old black and whites was astounding.

"William Powell," I said.

"Ah."

"*Thin Man*, of course."

"*Manhattan Melodrama*."

"Ah."

"Preston Sturges."

"You like Preston Sturges? Man, it's so hard to get anyone to share my enthusiasm."

"*Sullivan's Travels*, to my mind, is one of the truest statements about artistic integrity in American culture."

"I'm with you. *The Lady Eve*—he was way ahead of the

pack. *Miracle at Morgan's Creek*—how did they get away with that one?"

"How indeed."

"And, oh, what's the one begins in a bar, and it's told as a sort of myth—uh..."

"The Great McGinty."

"Yes! Wait—is that it?"

"I think so."

"Right."

"Cary Grant."

"Cary Grant, to me, was THE movie star, meaning, his style of acting and his personal charm and magnetism, were made for the screen. No one else so embodied what a movie star IS."

"Yes. And he, of course, had a lengthy career, but I think was better early on. Though some later color films, like his work with Hitchcock, are certainly worth talking about."

"Very funny film comic—he doesn't get enough credit. *Arsenic and Old Lace* or *Bringing Up Baby* or *His Girl Friday* or the underrated *Monkey Business*. He practically invented the double take."

"Right, or *The Bishop's Wife*."

"Uh huh. Charm, he oozed it. Think of another actor who oozed so much charm."

"Can't. The Wizard of Ooze."

"And then, perhaps his best film, *Holiday,* or the bleak *None But the Lonely Heart*."

"I haven't seen that last one."

"Go ye and seek it out. Grant disowned it, too close to his own life or something."

"Huh."

"Yeah."

"You get to watch movies in, uh, after you're—" It took me

a long time to get comfortable with the correct terminology about death and dying, about spiritual matters that I couldn't pretend to understand.

"Movies in the Afterlife? Ha. Of course, what would Heaven be if there were no screening rooms?"

"Heaven?"

"If you like."

"Then you came from Heaven."

"I made up the name. I don't know the name. But, the screening rooms of your dreams—no one talks. The popcorn is fresh as if God had just popped it in his Sempiternal Jiffy Pop."

"I get the feeling my leg is being pulled."

"Faith, son."

"Right."

"Heaven Can Wait."

"Uh—"

"The movie. The original."

"Right, right."

"James Mason."

"Almost as smooth as Cary Grant."

"In a way, yes. And he could play a villain, a slimy, smooth villain, which Grant, clearly did not wish to do."

"Maybe they never asked him to."

"Even Bogart played bad guys, unsympathetic characters, without hurting his star appeal."

"Early on, he did."

"No, no. I'm thinking of *In a Lonely Place*. Bad man."

"I don't know it."

"Friend, we should go watch movies until we can't watch movies no more." And here Richard did something which unhinged me every time. He laughed. And when he laughed he seemed to incandesce and flux like a special effect. It was a laugh to savor. As if his laugh sparked off the Empyrean anvil. To this day I miss it.

And on and on the discussion of movies went. It was clearly a passion of Richard's, and I shared it, though my experience was not as broad as his was.

I would get home at 3 or 4 a.m. from these confabs and there would be a message on my machine. Sometimes I would play it and sometimes I would erase it without playing it. When I played it it said, "Jack where are you? I miss you. Please call."

*The Rapist

Of course, Helen called me at the bookstore after numerous nights went by and I never called her back or explained my sudden absence from her life.

"Jack," her voice was tentative. She was frightened.

How could I have frightened poor Helen Holland? I was not, I believe I've already expatiated this, worth spit.

"Helen," I said. My voice was tired because I was tired and because I had nothing prepared to say to her. Woe to us when prepared statements become necessary.

"What's going on, Jack?" she said, and her voice splintered.

Oh perfidy! Oh, fie on humankind and its clumsy practitioners.

"Nothing," I said. So wise, so empathetic.

"When are we getting together? I miss you."

"I know," I said. Curse me. I know. Just what the passionate partner wants to hear. Like a therapist who says, I acknowledge your anger. To which the gulled and irate patient should answer, I'll acknowledge you right upside your Freudian head.

Helen was silent. I think she might have been crying.

"Tonight, dear," I said.

"Ok," Helen Holland said. Immediately she seemed better.

"Tonight, we'll rent something—how about an old Cary Grant?—and eat some junk food and have sex. What do you say?"

"Sounds wonderful," Helen Holland said. She was as gay as a schoolgirl.

"Ok," I said, as if I'd just proven myself a worldbeater in the romance domain.

That night Richard showed up just as I started my car. My headlights fixed him—either he had just materialized as I flicked them on, or he was standing there in the dark and I hadn't seen him—and he held a fringed arm up over his eyes.

"Get a beer?" he said, coming around to the driver's side window.

"Hop in," I said.

*Playing Dodgeball in the Upper Emotions

The next day there was hell to pay and rightfully so.

Helen called me while I was getting ready for work. I answered the phone with toothpaste in my mouth. Toothpaste and lies, I thought.

But, no, Helen deserved better.

"What the hell—" she began.

I became a dog on its back immediately. I was ready to admit to everything from infidelity to killing Jimmy Hoffa and hiding his body in the base of the Statue of Liberty.

"Helen—" I said, quickly, cutting off her destruction of my character. I was ready to destroy it for her.

"You deserve an explanation. I am a shit, a roundheel, a loser. I don't deserve you. Let me explain."

Therefore, I told Helen Holland that I was haunted. I told her everything—about my trip to San Francisco, which seemed a part of it, somehow. I omitted Sharilyn, of course. She didn't need to know about my lost love. I told her how Richard Brautigan began appearing to me, talking to me. I told her it was so unpredictable, that he would disappear for weeks and then reappear in my life, as steady as Old Time. He was a magician, this spook! And I was his willing galloglass.

Friends, Helen wasn't buying any of it.

"You ditch me and then tell me a lunatic tale as some sort of recompense. I don't believe it. Give me some credit, buddy. You don't love me, just say that in so many words, how about it?"

I was challenged. I could easily insert here the words that needed saying: I don't love you, Helen Holland, and I don't know why. You're beautiful, sexy and smart and I don't love you. Frankly, it's a mystery. I've thought long and hard about it. I find in my heart no love—perhaps that's it. There is no love in my heart, for you or for anyone. There is instead a Mohole there, an emptiness, a loblolly. Throw me away, don't look for me, I am a lost soul.

But I didn't say any of that.

Instead I said, ok, I will introduce you to my ghost.

*Cleopatra's Asp in the Clutter Called Us

That night, after work, Helen was waiting outside for me. We stood uneasily in the parking lot, shifting our respective weights to our respective feet. We were almost shy with each other.

The sodium lights made us look ghostly—there's an irony here for irony-spelunkers.

After about a half hour Helen looked at me the way Cleopatra must have looked at the victims of her asp.

"Where's your spook?" she asked.

"I told you. It's unpredictable. He'll come and then he won't. I can't count on him."

"But you can count on me," she said.

We both thought about those words for a second. I don't think it was exactly what Helen wanted to say but there it was, out there, for us to contemplate.

"Yes," I said, finally. "I can count on you, can't I?"

She smiled. It was a crack in her painted face.

"Let's go home," I said.

We went back to my place and *Double Indemnity* was on TNT. It was a benison.

After the movie, Helen looked at me and smiled sweetly. She kissed me wetly on the mouth. It was a goodbye kiss.

*He Lives!

But, friends, it was only goodbye for the night.

The next night, Helen again waited for me in the parking

lot.

"Hello," I said. The shy factor was still at work. The Bashful Scale was registering about 70%.

"Hello," she said, her arms across her chest either for warmth or protection.

"Well—" I started, when a voice from the shadows sent a shock into my bowels.

"Who is this lovely lady?" Richard Brautigan's ghost said.

He walked out of the wavering umbra by the trashcans near the back wall, his countenance like a balladmonger of old, as if in his holsters he carried loaded verse. Crambo Rambo!

"Richard!" I exclaimed. I was giddy like a teenager.

Helen Holland stared at the vision in front of her. There was no denying it was the late hippie poet from San Francisco.

"I'm Helen," she said.

Richard took her hand, a gallant knight. Helen was charmed down to her slender ankles.

"Shall we get some drinks?" Richard asked.

"Yes," I said, trying to get the happy puppy out of my voice.

The three of us went to The Sweet and Dangerous, a nearby watering hole, and we sat at a corner table and talked and talked, long into the whispering night. Richard was at his best, funny, sweet, courtly, wise and friendly. I was so proud of him I could have expectorated. My ghost, I kept thinking—foolish, fleshly vanity—my pal.

Richard listened intently as Helen talked of her favorite writers—Iris Murdoch, Sylvia Plath, Diana DiPrima.

"Diana, lovely woman," Richard said, somewhat wistfully.

Helen blushed—she forgot, in the heat of the trialogue, that she was talking to a literary legend.

"Do you write?" Richard said, wiping foam from his

mustache.

"In secret," Helen answered.

Secret indeed. It was the first I had heard of it. I felt a stab of jealousy, right here, beneath my sternum.

"But Jack's stuff is so much better. You've read it, of course?" Helen trilled.

Richard looked at me with a gunslinger's sly smile.

"Well, Jack," Richard said.

"I'll show you something," I said quickly, so as not to appear a doofus.

"Indeed you will," Richard said, and he put his large arm around my shoulders.

It was a warm night. An enchanted night.

***What Drives Us and How We Drive**

And the best part was that it didn't end in the Sweet and Dangerous.

We left Richard at the bar. He said he wanted to play "Mack the Knife" on the jukebox a few more times.

"Tomorrow, we talk poetry," he said, holding me with the Mariner's stare. He looked directly into my, um, soul.

"Ok," I said.

It was the first time that Richard had ever mentioned the future. He was in some control then of his time, of time itself.

"Ok," I said.

In the car driving home, Helen was the happiest I'd ever seen her. She was looking at me with long, liquefied looks. She had her hand on my thigh. It was warm, like young blood.

"Ah, Jack," she said.

I smiled encouragement her way. I wanted to get her home and into bed, while she was feeling this goopy. It had been a while since we had had sex—too long for my particularly satyric—not satiric—ways.

But it was not to be.

Because.

Because Helen Holland was moved, moved to amorous adventurism.

Her hand moved from my thigh to my crotch. She began to tenderly knead my balls and my cock responded the way cocks do. The Way Cocks Do.

"Mm," I said, trying to concentrate on the slate grey road, disappearing under our car, appearing in our headlights and then not.

Helen Holland unzipped my pants.

I helped her tug them down some.

My cock stood up like one of those terracotta soldiers. And it could have stood that long.

Helen manipulated it expertly with her sweet palm.

"Oh, oh," she cooed. "My haunted but hard as hell prick."

"Sweetheart," I said, my voice trundling between puffs of breath. "Save it for the bed. I want to…do you, too."

"No," she said. "This is all for you. This is for this night."

And she lowered her head into my lap, where it swam around like an otter. The road disappeared. It was an act of the strongest will to make it reappear.

Helen Holland sucked on me like she had never sucked on me before. It was a difference in quality, in quantity, in imagination. I came, friends, like the iceman. She swallowed, humming to herself as she did.

I had to pull the car over.

She raised her head and gave me a long, feline smirk.

"I love you," I said, and I kissed her mouth, that tasted of bleach and mushrooms. I tongued her and tasted myself.

"My goodness, Mr. Man," she said. "You've been deprived, haven't you? That was weeks of come."

"I guess so," I said. I was dizzy. I didn't think I could drive. I didn't think I could ever drive again.

"We'll have to make sure that you don't go that long without ever again," Helen Holland said.

It was quite a sentence.

It was a sentence.

*Chin-Chin at the Next Bardo

So began a series of evenings where the three of us would meet for colloquy and literary buzz. Helen, bless her, could talk books, and I think she charmed Richard no end. I even—God help me—read some of my poems aloud. Helen beamed. Richard was kind. He seemed so much happier discussing with Helen her current reading habits and opinions. He was smitten with her, in a way, though he was an honorable ghost and would not tread upon a friend's emotions.

Which begged the question, could a ghost make it with a human again? It was just curiosity on my part.

Later.

And, after these late night chin-chins, these meetings in the wee small hours, which sparked and smoked and boogied in and out of the light, Helen Holland loved me up good. She loved me like no one had loved me since Sharilyn. So I began to think about Sharilyn again. And that wasn't good.

I admit to being slightly obsessed with Sharilyn. She represented something for me—something I could not quite figure out. She was like adulthood, like a test for adulthood that I had somehow failed.

Silly, yes?

Yet there it was, a roadblock in my self-image. I wanted to talk to Sharilyn again and I wanted to ask her: what went wrong?

So many times in our lives, people flow in and out, and so many times we have no idea why. Wouldn't it be great if we could know the answers—know why some people stuck (stick) and some didn't (don't)?

This is what I wished, an imprudent aspiration.

Yet, I thought, I had a direct line to the afterlife. Perhaps the answer was not so far away. I knew a ghost. I was a ghost's intimate.

***The Double-Bed Dream Gallows**

For months this went on.

Lively conversation, lively sex.

Who would be fool enough not to relish such a period in one's life?

But, instead, I wanted Sharilyn. And, while, I was in bed with Helen, I was picturing Sharilyn, her willowy beige body uncoiling over me with colubrine sensuality. God forgive me, Helen, when your golden head was bent over my manhood I was picturing a woman with chocolate hair, a woman who performed just such a task, many many moons ago. I closed my eyes and felt myself come in Sharilyn Chwedyk's warm, dark mouth.

Distracted, distended, strung out on the wire of remembrance, I was no boyfriend. I was not even that good a lover.

Did Helen Holland sense that something was wrong? That her loverboy was elsewhere, that the body beneath her was also in San Francisco?

Pity us poor earthlings. Never content with what we have. Constantly seeking more, constantly wishing that every loose end in our lives be gathered up and given meaning.

But, friends, let's stay with Helen a while.

I see now they were golden days. Let's honor them by keeping the story there for a while. Ah, Helen, Ah, humanity!

***Sharilyn Again, Again, Again**

Then, abruptly, Richard stopped appearing.

The first night Helen and I shrugged, went home, watched *Island of Lost Souls* on Turner Classic Movies. We made love, but, my beloved confidants, there was something missing. I mean, we both had our orgasms, and let's not take any orgasm for granted, but, compared with the previous weeks' couplings, this was uninspired, sex by rote.

You understand why.

I think at the time even I understood why.

The next night Richard again didn't show and Helen said

that she had the cramps and would just as soon go home to bed anyway.

I slept alone. I almost relished it.

I missed Richard. I missed Sharilyn.

***Not Chinese**

The next night Helen didn't show up at all. I didn't care.

I called her in the morning and she acted as if it wasn't strange, this separation, this silence.

God spare us all from such silences, such denials.

I said: "Helen, we are all alone."

She thought I meant, still, even then, that she and I were alone. Together.

I meant to get at the invisible things between us, the unspoken Twentieth Century, the way nights slide into day like a coffin being lowered into its hole, the ghosts. I meant to get at so much, and I was foolish to think that such a small, homely phrase could carry all that weight.

"Sometimes alone is a strong bond," Helen Holland said, after a while.

"Hm," I answered.

"I'll come by tonight. What time do you get off work?"

"I don't work tonight," I said, in the cardboard play in which we were cast.

"I'll come by around 6:30 and bring dinner."

"Ok."

"Chinese?"

"No, not Chinese."

"You love Chinese."

"Yes."

"Ok, not Chinese. Maybe I'll cook."

"Ok."

*The Night of the Troublesome Indian Olio

That night Helen brought a stew, an olio of exotic spices, in a crockpot. When she entered the house she was cursing and her left pant leg was dripping with something oddly dyed and aromatic.

"Damn thing overturned in the car. I tried to rescue it with my foot."

"Ah."

"Can you take it please?" Helen said, shouldering past me on her way to the bathroom.

I looked stupidly into the pot. It was sort of red, sort of yellow.

It smelled like Indian.

Helen emerged from the bathroom, her face still set in irritated consternation.

"Put the damn crockpot in the kitchen. Plug the fucking thing in," she said.

I did as I was told.

I came back and sat beside Helen Holland on the couch.

She was wearing a black cloud like a funny hat.

But it wasn't funny, not even to me, who can find humor, normally always, most times, in other people's misfortunes.

She stared straight ahead.

A long, deadly silence ensued.

It was the silence of a battlefield after the battle. We were both counting our dead.

"Smells good," I said, presently.

Helen burst into sobs and fell against me.

"You don't love me," she said.

A bad dithering now commenced. It was a dithering like God's before an earthquake.

"I know," I said.

Damn me, that's what I said.

Helen stopped crying but began keening, in small bursts, into my shirt collar.

She had turned her water into whine.

We held each other for a few more minutes. Helen was warm against me, even as she became a bag full of sharp tools, garden implements, picks and adzes and axes.

When she left she didn't even stop to get her stew.

I wanted the name of it.

I ate it in silence, leafing through an *American Poetry Review*.

When I was finished I flushed the leftover stew down the disposal.

I still wanted to name it, even as it washed away, down down down, into the vast American sewer system, the end result of our best and worst aspirations. Our dreams of an acceptable Heaven.

*Norm Knows

Weeks passed.

Norm called.

"How's Helen?" he invariably asked in an early version.

"Gone like the Loggerhead Turtle. Gone like the Galapagos Flightless Cormorant. Gone like the dodo."

"I get it."

"Gone."

"What—"

"A study in gone."

"What—"

"Don't ask what or why, my friend. There is no what or why. Humans don't stick."

"Right."

"Besides I didn't love her. I wanted to, really. She was inexpressibly sweet and sexy and smart—"

"I hate that."

"I know."

"She's gone."

"That's what I'm saying."

"So, now, if I know you, you're through with women."

I hung up. I forgot to ask Norm about Donna. I'm too solipsistic.

*LVMM's Bear Carcass

I had to have a similar conversation with Lovely Vita Meter Maid.

The difference being that LVMM had a dead marriage on her hands, as unwieldy a construct as a bear carcass or an architectural model for The Universum Science Center.

"How's Helen?" Vita asked, her voice reduced to a rasp worthy of Mercedes McCambridge, from woe, from life weariness.

"You ok?" I couldn't help but ask.

"Sure."

"Helen's gone."

"Really?"

"As gone as—"

"Don't."

"Sorry."

"She left you. She left you because you wouldn't commit. She left you because even when you said 'I love you' she knew you were acting, faking it. She left you because men are base amateurs with the deeper emotions."

"Ok, Lovely Vita."

"I don't feel so pretty."

"You're the prettiest woman I know," I said like a schoolboy, except that it was true and she knew it and between us there had always been that understanding.

I could hear soft sobbing.

"I'm sorry," I said again.

"Find me an apartment," Lovely Vita Meter Maid said. "Find me a new life."

***Norm Runs the Voodoo Down**

Norm called again.

"What are you doing today?'

"Coughing up hair balls."

"Alrighty. Then you're up for some tennis?"

"No."

"What are you up for?"

"What am I up for? Damn, that is the question."

"Second-hand record shopping?"

"No."

"I shouldn't continue listing activities, should I, because you'd let me continue listing activities so that you could say 'no' in that deadpan way and by doing so reduce me to the friend who tries to cheer the other friend up, the other friend essentially cheerless and incapable of human interaction? Right?"

"No."

(Donna?)

***The Recipe To Turn Off Your Brain**

After spending all my days either at the bookstore, where I walked the aisles like one of the undead, handing out Jackie Collins novels like candy, recommending Flann O'Brien to suburban housewives who won't understand a word of him, pushing Pushkin on highschoolers, or at home, where I watched bad TV, *The Jeffersons, The Price is Right, The Man from Atlantis*, or bad old movies, *Trog, How to Stuff a Wild Bikini, The Reincarnation of*

Peter Proud, and ate bad food—Mexican TV dinners seemed to be the most appropriate victuals—after days of this, my mind turned off. Just like throwing a switch. So, there it is, the recipe for turning your brain off. You may follow it when you are wretched, when you are one of the great unhealthy, when your puzzle piece no longer fits into the big picture. You saw it here first.

*He Says It Anyway

Norm called.

"Listen—" he began.

I cut him off with a scimitar screech.

"Norm—" I fairly shouted into the phone.

"Fuck me—" Norm said.

"Norm, listen, I've made a decision. I need to tell you something. Something that will perhaps explain a lot to you, if not everything."

"This is gonna be good. It's a Moonie kind of thing, am I right?"

"No."

"Ok."

"Norm, my oldest friend, listen to me now."

My hands were sweating. My brow felt clammy. Maybe I was getting sick. From lack of sunshine vitamins.

"I'm haunted by the ghost of the late hippie writer, Richard Brautigan."

I liked the sound of that phrase, containing as it did, so much truth.

Norm was uncharacteristically silent.

He was not calling me a bullshitter. This was a good sign.

"So Vita was right," he said.

"Yes."

"What now?"

"Well, I don't know. I haven't seen Richard in weeks…"

"You call him Richard."

"Well, we've gotten close."

"And he's dead."

"As the ropes of roses on St. James Street. As my relationship with Helen Holland."

"Is he—what do I want to ask?—semi-transparent?"

"No."

"How did this begin? Why is he haunting a bookstore clerk in Oklahoma City?"

"I don't know. He doesn't know. Perhaps together we will figure it out."

"You and Richard Brautigan."

"Yes."

"Ok, buddy."

"You're with me on this, then?"

"Sure," Norm said, but he was reserving the right to summon the guys in the white coats.

"When can I meet him?" Norm said now, weakly.

"I don't know. I don't know what will happen next. Everything is so confusing. There's the relationship with Helen which seemed, briefly, to have something to do with Richard's appearances and disappearances. There's Lovely Vita Meter Maid, whose heart is diminishing at the same rate her voice is. Soon, she will be a whisperwill. We need to get her away from that husband of hers. He's made of Portland Cement, Norm. He's not a real man."

"You're raving."

"No."

"He's moved out on her."

"He keeps coming back, apparently. We need to—you fill in the blank."

"Break his legs."

"There you go."

"Hamstring him."

"Ok."

"You're mad."

"And then there's that. I feel, sometimes, like I'm not pure, not sane enough to conjure my friendly ghost."

"Right. Like Caspar."

"And then there's Sharilyn, who haunts me as thoroughly as Richard does."

"The chick in San Francisco."

"Oh," I moaned.

"And, buddy, listen to me now. This may not be the best time to tell you this. I've been meaning to, but—"

"Don't, " I said, holding up an admonishing hand.

"Lovely Vita Meter Maid is in love with you."

*Lark Calls with a Joke (3)

First Joy calls. She wants to know who this new woman is I'm in love with. I have no idea whom she's talking about. Is it whom?

How did she hear about Helen Holland? Or is she talking about LVMM?

I expect my mother to call next. They usually come in pairs like animals for the ark. She does not.

My father calls. First he talks about the weather, then he asks me if I need money. Dad. I love the old stoic.

Lark calls.

"Hello?" I inquire.

"Bill Gates is hanging out with the chairman of General Motors. 'If automotive technology had kept pace with computer technology over the past few decades,' boasts Gates, 'you would now be driving a V-32 instead of a V-8, and it would have a top speed of 10,000 miles per hour. Or, you could have an economy car that weighs 30 pounds and gets a thousand miles to a gallon of gas. In either case, the sticker price of a new car would be less than $50.'

'Sure,' says the GM chairman. 'But would you really want to drive a car that crashes four times a day?'"

It's never imperative—in fact, I'd advise against—that one answers Lark. When the joke is over he hangs up.

FIVE: Following Richard Brautigan (I mean it this time)

*It Was Raining a Motherfucker

It was raining a motherfucker.

It was raining a Dostoyevsky novel.

It was raining a Kurosawa film.

It was raining a Trout Mask Replica.

Through the sheets of water, like a curtain hung over my perception, I could make out a car.

I got into this car.

I owned the car, the car seen dimly through the cascades of water.

Through the windshield of the car, which was my car, the rain seemed worse. I felt as if I were inside someone, inside another human being, and only barely able to see through his or her eyes. He or she was crying. This was causing the blurring effect, tears. I asked him or her to stop crying so that I could see and drive.

I did not want to drive in the motherfucker.

I wanted to be able to see.

In the rain.

I don't know how I did it but I saw another car alongside me.

I don't know how I knew who was driving.

I only knew I was happy Richard was back and I no longer cared about the rain that was a motherfucker.

*We Were All Moving and a Slit in the Watermelon Sky

In the back seat of my car there was a bag, a bag packed for a short trip. This was because I was planning to take a short trip, sometime, sometime in the next few days. The reason for this sudden excursion should be obvious—I was running away from Helen Holland. I was a heartbreaker and I hated myself. Therefore, I wanted to flee.

I am not proud of this. Understand that.

So, I sat in this rainstorm to end all rainstorms, and gazed out through God's tears, and I thought, there goes Richard Brautigan. He did not look my way. Yet, I should follow him. Where is he going? What could a ghost have to do? In addition, where did a ghost get a car?

I pulled into traffic behind him.

We drove down West Concordia—I could see fast food signs and motel signs and car dealership signs, lights in the dim.

The only humans in sight were in the most proximate cars.

We were all moving, moving westward, watched over by machines of loving grace.

When I figured out that Richard's car was heading for I-40 my heart gave a small lurch. This is the route I took originally to find Richard Brautigan. Something clicked as if everything before this was preparation, preparation for this voyage westward.

We both took the on-ramp. It was as if I were attached to him by an invisible cord—my car pulled onward by his. U r g e n t uncanny umbilicus!

The rain began to let up—somewhere off to the South I could see a wee sliver of sunshine, a slit in the clouds like a slice in a watermelon.

A blessing.

In August.

*I Felt Like the Car Was Driving Me

As we drove I began to wonder if Richard even knew I was there. My car followed his as if it were under the influence of a particularly strong magnet. And I was the unwitting slave of its necromantic horsepower.

I felt like the car was driving me.

I imagine I was steering. I imagine this.

And, just when I was convinced that I was alone in my powerlessness, adrift on the great ocean of the American highway system, being led by a ghost who was unaware of my presence, Richard looked in his rear view mirror and smiled.

His face was lit as if on a screen, as if an actor in that comedy called America, and his eyes locked on mine.

His gaze said, *Follow*.

Just follow and we shall see what we shall see.

There seemed to be a purpose in this, a reasoning that was beyond my ken, yet held me as if I were a sleepwalker. I needed a purpose. Why?

*Put the Book Down

We drove past town after town, Richard occasionally espying me in his mirror, his smile a reassurance in the tricky world of travel.

We passed towns, ticking them off like chapters in a book.

I travel this way. I think of the time as reading time—every hundred miles is like a hundred pages. Traveling, say, at 60 miles per hour, you do a mile a minute. Moreover, the average page in a book takes about a minute to read. 100 miles = 100 pages. It works. It helps make a trip seem more of an accomplishment. And, when finished, you have, in your head, another world, the world of the author, the world of the highway, which is built of concrete and dreamstuff and little towns like authorial asides. Like digression.

Chapters we ticked off as we proceeded in our abstracted journey:

Weatherford

Clinton

Foss

Elk City (one of my favorite digressions—makes one want to read its story, doesn't it?)

Texola (on the border between Part One of the book and Part Two: Texas)

PART TWO

Twitty (ah, Twitty, we only stopped for gas, and there, in your comfortable nest of a town, there exists something on the endangered species list, a full-service gas station. I was looking forward to Richard getting out of his car, just so I could see him again whole, stretching his long ghost legs, slapping his floppy hat on his thigh. And, when I paid for my gas, Burt, the attendant smiled a Texas smile at me, and said, Good Trip, as if he understood it all, the haunting, the desire to leave behind things which confuse and betray, the whole admixture of life, in its pied beauty—but, perhaps, I read too much into Burt, bewhiskered and toothy, a roadside angel.)

Shamrock (I couldn't make this up—read the book, Interstate Forty West.)

Alanreed

McLean

Groom

Lark (my brother's town!)

Claude

Panhandle

And the addendum, boxed and asterisked, the turnoff to the town of Canyon, the one we only glanced down, the Road Not Taken.

Instead we arrived at our first stop, Amarillo.

Put the book down, it's time to rest your eyes. Life outside the book awaits. What will happen? Put the book down, children.

Let life back in.

*She Had That Amarillo Brillo

Richard pulled his old Buick LeSabre—it looked like my grandfather's car—into a roadside inn. It was one of those non-descript access-road stops, owned by some family with sons who didn't graduate high school and daughters who entered the local beauty pageants because their mother had been a Queen in her day.

One is tempted to call it a No Name Motel, yet this 50s era inn was called Little Arcady. Which made Richard a happy haint.

I sat in my car as he went into the office. He emerged and headed toward me.

"I got a double. You are stopping with me, right?" He had that air about him, the assumption that you would follow him into hell.

The Hippie Hegemon.

"Richard, what are we doing?" I felt it important that I ask.

"We are seeking Paradise, friend. And, look, already we have found a little Arcady." He smiled his smile, charming in life, charming in death.

When we unlocked room 106, it was as I had imagined it.

Horrible, polyester counterpanes over wooden beds. Horrible, mass-produced art. A cramped bathroom, with grouty tiles. And, from the same adjuvant elves who must work with the Gideons: Magic Fingers! On both beds!

I have a theory that Magic Fingers are part of the Gideon's secret plot to make the highway a place of marvel and awe and the kind of wonderment Old Testament characters took for granted, eating it up with their morning manna and fruit.

Richard tossed an old dusty Gladstone onto the desk, next to the RCA. And he threw his long body onto one of the rigid beds. He looked immediately comfortable.

I sat on the other bed.

"Magic Fingers," I mumbled.

Richard's eyes brightened, an adamantine glint, like a gem.

"The desk clerk asked if we wanted women," he said, slyly.

"Women," I repeated dumbly. I was stuck in my role: follower.

"Company is actually the way he put it."

"What did you say?"

"Well, hell, Jack, I said, of course. I said, naturally, and I meant naturally because it's a natural thing, this need to rut, this commingling of the feminine and the masculine. This thing called fucking." And he laughed a horse laugh at his own good joke.

I had to smile.

I also had to pee and then call Oklahoma City to tell someone where I was. So I could believe it.

"You're where?" Norm said.

"Amarillo," I said, deadpan—I was looking for emotion back; I wasn't giving it.

"Texas?"

"No, Amarillo, West Germany. Yeah, Texas. This is where Richard stopped, so it's where I stopped. We've got a little room here for the night."

Richard was engrossed in *Wheel of Fortune* on the crappy TV. He wasn't hearing me.

"Um, Jack. Why?"

"I don't know. I had to leave. I had to follow."

"Uh huh."

"Is everything ok back there? I know I left in a rush."

"Sure. We're not gonna collapse because you're gone."

"Thanks."

"Yeah. Listen. You ought to call Vita."

"And Helen, yeah, sure," I said.

"Helen?" Norm asked.

The fact that Norm didn't call her Lovely Vita Meter Maid meant something. I wanted to know what.

Vita picked up on the first ring as if she were waiting for a call from the governor to stay the execution.

"Oh, Jack, I'm so happy it's you. Where are you, my sweet?"

Vita called me 'her sweet.' This meant something too. This meant too much. I didn't know how to proceed.

"You ok?"

"Sure, sure."

"Uh, I won't be back for a while…"

"Oh, really?" She sounded like a disappointed little girl.

"Vita, uh, this is Jack. Your old compadre. What's going on?"

"Jack," she said, her voice husky with emotion. "Jack…"

I waited. There was now something between LVMM and her old compadre. It was already there without her finishing her thought. I felt it moving in like a weather system.

"Jack," she said for the third time. "I think I'm in—"

And that's when the girls knocked on the door. Loud knocks. Rambunctious, playful, sexy knocks. They obliterated Wheel of Fortune. They obliterated Magic Fingers and bad art and prickly bedclothes.

They obliterated the end of Lovely Vita's confession.

"What's that?" she said.

"Um, guests. Listen—"

Richard opened the door. In stepped two young women—God help us I hope they were 18—dressed like Daisy Mae, and grinning as if we were their next meal. In a sense we were.

"I'll call you again. Sorry."

"When Jack?" Vita's voice semi-quavered.

"Next stop. Promise."

By the time I hung up Richard had already chosen our respective mates.

One of the two, the plumper, rounder of the two, came and sat down on the bed next to me. Richard's, a tall, leggy blond, who looked a little like the actress Daryl Hannah, was already on top of him—their lengths matched like Lincoln Logs—her tongue in his mouth, his hands on her ass.

"Jilly," the little round demirep next to me said.

"What?" I countered. I thought this was some sort of question, a test perhaps before we could begin.

"My name is Jilly," she said. She undid a button on her ridiculous shirt, tied in a knot under her ample bosom.

"Ah, Jilly," I said. "Richard."

She screwed up her wholesome, puckish face.

"I thought he was Richard."

"Oh, yes, well, we're, ha ha, oddly enough, both named Richard."

"Oh," she giggled.

She fairly ripped open her shirt now and her bra could barely contain her bulge.

"Oh," I said. Which was preamble enough for Jilly. She leapt upon me, simultaneously removing her bra, a pretty good trick.

She really had the nicest breasts. Very round with almost no nipples.

Her upper body was salted with wee whiteheads.

And when we were both naked I found something else about her memorable. Her pubic hair was a dark tangle, like the roots of the Bo-Tree, like wire. And, with the sounds of Richard and Letty next to me, and the sight of Letty's long, white, blond body on top of my ghostly compatriot, not to mention the profusion that was Jilly, I was as aroused as I've ever been.

It was quite a show.

Afterwards, Letty and Jilly, absurd monikers, lay facing each other and began a conversation as if we were not even there.

Richard negotiated the women's payment—where does a ghost get money?—and afterwards told me that they were the motel owner's daughters.

What a world.

We ordered room service—soggy club sandwiches—and watched *The Sterile Cuckoo* on TV. Richard seemed delighted by the film—I know John Nichols, he said, a good storyteller—and I was too dizzy to ask for simple directions, such as where are we going, what are we doing. Is there life after death? How does an incorporeal body enter a corporeal one?

That night I did not sleep well. I moved in and out of a dream that featured wild farm girls who turned into animals at will and a wavering specter that was sometimes Richard and sometimes Vita.

I woke up the next morning with a headache bigger than my head.

*Pity the Morning Light That Refuses To Wait for Dawn

I lay in the grey, sink colored light and pondered my decision to take to the road, so precipitously, so unlike me. As I lay there, the light creeping around the poor curtains, the morning a bright wound that suppurated behind my eyes, I gradually became aware of being alone.

"Richard?" I said.

I got up—the bathroom was empty.

Perhaps he had gone to breakfast. I dressed as quickly as I could.

When I opened the door, the day hit me like a savage at his altar.

I squinted, put a hand up, scout-wise, above my eyes.

Richard's car was gone!

Immediate panic choked me. I took a step outside.

Then I saw him. Sitting at the edge of the lot, looking slightly back over his shoulder, apparently waiting for me. Or was he? Maybe he was just leaving, abandoning me—what proof did I have that he was traveling for or with me?

I ran back inside, threw everything into my suitcase. I just knew that when I went back outside he would be gone. And I'd be stuck in Amarillo, Texas, with a headache and a sore crotch from last night's calisthenics.

But, no, he was still there!

I threw my bag into the back seat and started my car. Was the bill paid? Were we skipping out? I couldn't bother with such details.

And just as I backed out, Richard's car rolled out of the parking lot onto the access road, heading westward back toward the campestral novel, accordioning like a popup book, that is I-40.

*The Richard Brautigan Bivehicular Poltergeist Procession

We were moving again.

I was glued to Richard's bumper—I had it memorized like my name, address, and phone number when I was a kid, in case I wandered outside of my parent's sphere of influence. Richard's rusty bumper—I memorized even the oxidized spots, like a Rorschach denoting something chthonic—had two bumper stickers: Impeach Nixon and Frodo Lives. It made it easy to stay in line behind him. Also, there weren't any other cars on the road the color of Richard's car—a sort of once-Gumby-green, now Pokey-Orange.

We were moving again.

I was reading again. Mileposts were page numbers, municipalities the place where I put my bookmark to take a breath.

Vega

Adrian

And the chapter on the border of Part Two and Part Three: Glenrio.

San Jon

And a long area—white on the map—a part of the story that's just illustration, something by Wyeth perhaps, or Frederic Remington. The road was like a snake lying in the sun. The surrounded scenery carried past us by muscular angels.

And then: Tucumcari.

Who approaching it cannot begin singing "Willin'?" Say the word: Tucumcari. A poet's city, a place for The Richard Brautigan Bivehicular Poltergeist Procession to pull over and reassess, reconnoiter, re-energize.

Which we did.

*Hot as Monkeys

There's no sun like desert sun.

It was as if the air had fainted, the sun pomped and circumstanced.

It made rings around the smallest glass.

It was hot as monkeys, hot as a black pudding.

Richard seemed to relish it. He took off his hat, leaning against his Buick, in the parking lot of a Stuckey's, just outside

Tucumcari.

He waved the hat around like a cowboy, like a cow swishing flies.

"Heat," he said, as if he had discovered it.

"We gonna stay here?" I asked. So concrete, so neurotic—I was a carp, a smudge on the painting Richard was working on.

"Hm," he said.

"Lunch anyway," I said, as if I had a vote.

"Ah, Lunch," Richard said. "The midday meal. Yes!" He pointed a finger upward in a Eureka pose.

"I just realized I missed breakfast," I whined.

"Brunch!" Richard said now, his eyes demon-bright.

***Brunch in Tucumcari**

Pancakes with Vermont! syrup

Link sausages

Eggs Benedict Arnold (well, that's what the menu said—I can't figure the link between this dusty New Mexico town and the Traitor)

Toast (wheat and white)

Pot of coffee (on the table)

*The Dead Are Good Listeners

"So, my man," Richard said, settling back in his chair. He lit up a cigarette and exhaled dramatically. "What's going on in your life that you would take to the road without preamble?"

"Richard," I said, stalling. I looked deep into his eyes, which were gentle, like a child's. "Women."

"A topic!"

"There's this woman, I mean, she's everything you'd want in a mate, you know, sexy and funny and kind and a great conversationalist."

"Sounds horrible. Helen."

"Well, yes, Helen…"

"She is all that. She's stuff."

"Yes, she is."

"But?"

"Well, I can't love her. I just don't. My emotions are frozen, locked away and forgotten, like the letters my father wrote my mother from The European Theater."

"Presumable, you've loved before."

"Yes."

"So, what's different now?"

"I don't know. I may be spent. I may be still hung up on this woman in San Francisco, who spurned me. Helen just may not be right for me."

"Tell me about this woman in San Francisco."

So I told him the story of Sharilyn Chwedyk. It was a long story and I embellished it with emotional crepe. Richard, I must say this for the old dead man, was a damn good listener.

*Oh and By the Way

"Oh and by the way," Richard said at the conclusion of our repast. "I'm being followed. Nothing to worry about."

*Because When the End Comes You Are Alone

Richard and I, sated on greasy breakfast foods, could not decide whether we wanted to explore Tucumcari—just why did it end up in that song? just for its euphonious name?—or climb back onto the slab and steer into a new chapter.

And, I did ask, dear reader, why we were a caravan? Why two cars and not the companionship of the voyage?

And here's Richard's cryptic answer:

"Because when the end comes you are alone."

This frightened (frightens) me.

*Somewhere Off to the South of Us Roswell Was Sending Brainwaves

Somewhere off to the south of us Roswell, New Mexico, was sending us brainwaves, messages in electronic impulses, from alien civilizations, far older than ours, civilizations that had risen and fallen, risen and fallen, until even Earth looked appetizing.

But, that is another novel.

Sorry.

***So I'll Travel Along with a Friend and a Song**

We started a new chapter.

I pulled in behind his Buick—after we had refueled—Frodo Lives!—and we swung into the story as if we alone could write it, without God, without our forebears, without preface or introduction or table of contents.

Here we go!

Montoya

Newkirk

Cuervo

Santa Rosa

lunch at Stuckey's

Clines Corner (I could see Richard craning his neck to look down the exit ramp for just a glimpse of a town called Clines Corner and I could imagine him cogitating on the quaintness of it, the Richardbrautiganness of it, and wondering, perhaps aloud, just who Cline is and why he has his own corner, but, it was just a passing fancy, a glim off our windshields, for we motored on, Cline's Corner only a flickering flame, memorialized only here, and only in our imaginations)

Moriarty (!)

Edgewood

Stanley (!)

Cedar Crest, just on the outskirts of:

Albuquerque!

Which may turn out to be the name of our next chapter.

***Albuquerque!**

New Mexico's largest city! Population Three Hundred and Thirty One Thousand Seven Hundred and Sixty Seven. Not Sixty Eight, my friends, No, this is precise. This is science instead of art.

Ignore it.

Albuquerque held us in its sway. It was here we stopped. This was to be a real visit, a plateau, a resting place for body/mind. An apex on our sine curve. Richard pulled into a Days Inn as if he had a reservation, and when he emerged from the office, he grinned as Jupiter on Juno grins. He held up a key and jingled it as if it were a bell.

Calling me to our room.

I parked next to Richard's Buick. I gave the traveler's stretch to indicate that we had stopped. To indicate that I was a traveler, a man comfortable with the road, the country, the world.

Our room number, even though it was a ground floor room, was 666.

***The Sunshine Building and Where To Get Your Kicks**

After freshening up, we both got into Richard's Buick and began to explore our new city. What were we in search of? Nothing so glamorous as the heart of America, pilgrims. We were in search of a good restaurant, a hip place where there might be comely young women and searing Mexican food.

We went downtown, a dusty, brown, little downtown, with few tall buildings, as if the Tower of Babel chastened Albuquerquians. We stopped briefly in front of an edifice called The Sunshine Building (!) and Richard spent an inordinate amount of time marveling at it.

"Such stately architectural whimsy," Richard said, with a far-away smile.

"Do you know much about architecture," I ventured, trying to keep up my end of the conversation.

Richard fixed me with a fishy eye. A troutfishinginamerica eye.

"No," he mumbled, getting back into the Buick and steering us down Central Avenue, which seemed to be, well, Central to the city. The Main Drag.

And, here was our brief epiphany: Central Avenue is really Route 66. As in get your kicks on.

We took it as an augury.

***If Here Are Eloi We Must Be Morlocks**

Shortly, we found the campus of the University of New

Mexico. It had a sort of plaza that faced onto Central. And there were the Eloi, the beautiful young people, without whom this old world would be an oily, black marble.

Women were everywhere—so much stimuli that one's member stood up just in tribute, straining at the front of your person, angling for the dry heat surrounding. And they were all striking, as radiant as doth the yonge sonne that in the ram hath foure degrees y-ronne.

Richard was split open like a fruit.

He moved forward in a daze, his cowboy coat flapping about him like wings. He really looked like a man from another time—well, he was, of course, but as I watched him move away from me, I thought of Quantrill or maybe John Brown.

And damned if he didn't stop one bright young thing and hold her in his gaze, as if he were the Ancient Mariner or a snake-charmer.

I skipped to catch up.

"…and are you native to this fair city," Richard was finishing.

The sinuous blond woman smiled like a Miles Davis solo.

"Yes," she said.

"But you go to the University here, also," Richard said. There was an unmistakable charm about the man, even given his basic goofiness and the fact that he was dead.

"No, no, I was just here to check out the movie schedule," she said.

"Movies?" Richard beamed.

"Yeah, tonight they're showing *La Strada*. Do you like the movies?"

"Ah, yes," Richard said. "Fellini." And there was that dreamy expression again, Richard in Cloudcuckooland.

There was a break in proceedings. A silence fell over us,

like the fearful calm that slumbers in the storm's portentous pause.

Finally, I stepped up to the plate and stuck out my hand.

"Jack," I said.

The Eloi put her soft paw into my hand, no so much a shake as a gift, a flower.

"Sue. Sue Generous," she said.

"This spectre here, this is Richard," I said.

"Richard," Sue said, switching her gift from me to him.

"Ah, Ms. Generous," he said. I thought he was about to kiss her hand, but instead he moved his Ulysses-like gaze back and forth between Sue and me.

"What are you boys doing?" Sue asked, a twinkle to her twaddle.

Sue had a thorn and rose tattoo engirdling her fine, fleshy biceps.

"Exploring," Richard said, a comedian's delivery.

"Want to join our party?" I said. I have no idea where that came from.

Sue hesitated. "Sure," she said. Then those magic words: "I have a friend."

***Sue Takes the Boys to The Frontier**

After ambulating a bit—the campus is beautiful, a sort of oasis in the crummy surrounding town, which is built with little imagination and little variance. So many houses look alike, so many streets like Anytown, USA. We were told numerous times during our stay in Albuquerque that we really ought to see Santa Fe. As if in apology for their second-rate status next to their more appealing neighboring town to the north.

As the sun went red in the west our attentions turned to eating.

Sue had stopped at a pay phone on campus to call her friend and she told her to meet us at a hot little diner called The Frontier. It apparently took some convincing because Sue was a long time on that phone call and her voice grew strident and even from a few yards away we could pick up the words "cute" and "eccentric."

We surmised whom the adjectives meant and there were no hard feelings.

Sue returned to us and I looked at her whole. Sue Generous had a wide white face with features carved on it so delicately they seemed ephemeral, fragile. And bangs—like a beach bunny, like Sue Lyon, or Carol Linley. She was a beach bunny in a city without a beach and this made her mysterious, almost like a poltergeist herself. I was immediately drawn to her, her warmth, and the almost moist aura that seemed to float off her pallid skin. Her white hair showed red roots, like a ghost image, pentimento.

The Frontier is the place to go in Albuquerque. Counter service. Large, boisterous crowds, fluorescent lighting that made you feel as if you were in a greenhouse. Famous for their sweet rolls.

While we waited to approach the counter, Sue's friend, Isabel, arrived. Isabel was about five foot five, as dark as Sue was light, heavy into eye makeup, and as shapely as a flame. Her breasts swelled like the sea in surge. They were breasts that you could not ignore. They defined Isabel and she, to her credit, acknowledged them and simultaneously rose above them. Richard was like a puppy.

"Hello," he said, his voice warm as honey oozed from top-most rocks.

Something had occurred. Something that Richard understood instantly and myself slowly. Richard had paired me with Sue—he practically tied the bow—and he had been waiting anxiously for her friend, in the hopes that he and she would be simpatico and that she would be an engine of human desire. One could see he was pleased.

However, it also left me and Sue in an awkward space/time warp. We seemed to be standing together in public view. Perhaps this is fancy on my part. But, no, Sue felt it too, I could see it in her body language, crossed arms, an expectant look, and finally, a gaze that went inside my eyes and rattled around in my head for a while, making assessments, the way one does when one visits someone's house and the bookcase beckons for inspection.

And, lo, Sue found me worthy. And I her.

But I get ahead of myself. We must eat.

We stepped into line. Sue was next to me, her fine, furry, thornéd arm brushed mine repeatedly. We were like friendly seals.

Smiling like bantlings.

"What should I eat?" I asked her. So that we would be human, see? Speech.

"Red or green," she said as we moved forward.

"Red or green what?'

"Chili, Dopey-mopey." She called me 'Dopey-mopey.' I was in love.

"Green chili?"

"Or red."

"I think I've seen green chili. Back home. In Oklahoma City. I think." I was speaking in short declarative sentences, rat-a-tat, God knows why.

Behind us there was snuffling and giggling and I glanced backwards to see Richard bending way over—he was a very tall ghost—and Eskimo-kissing the lovely Isabel, in that silky place women have between their neck and shoulder. Isabel was cooing. Things move quickly for the nosferatu, I thought.

Suddenly we were at the counter.

"Red," Sue was saying. "And some rolls. And a Coke. And, um, half a turkey sandwich with sprouts."

Her order was a poem. It was intimidating.

"Uh, hers is with mine," I said, my heart bumping with too high octane. "I'll try green chili and, uh, rolls, some ice tea, and the, uh, chicken appetizer."

Sue looked at me with bright, kittycat eyes. I had done alright. And when I paid she neither made a reach for her own wallet nor thanked me for stepping in. A notion had been busy being born and it seemed to be fine with both of us.

The food was delicious. Especially the rolls that seemed to have been made with honey and sand. I mean that in a good way.

"Do you boys—" and I loved Sue calling us boys—"want to see the Fellini."

"Most assuredly," Richard said, and before rising from where we ate, he kissed Isabel long and wet upon her mouth. The temperature had risen. The stakes were higher.

And in that glorious moment—that moment you understand that the evening will hold some fine discovering, some sweet intimacies, oh sweet moment unlike anything else in the long voyage, Life—in that moment I saw two faces before me, flickering like a magic lantern. One belonged to Sharilyn soft, brown visage like a seraph made of Eden's dust—and the other, readers, belong to Lovely Vita Meter Maid. And her dreamface was crying.

*Mr. Fellini and His Adult Fairy Tale About the Child-Woman Gelsomina

Afterwards the four of us sat in our uncomfortable seats in the makeshift screening room, even as the other participants in the showing moved on.

A dew fell upon us. Perhaps it was Poppy Snow.

Finally, Richard shook his golden hippie head.

"Fellini," he said.

After another moment passed we began to rise. Richard's earnest words arrested us.

"Thank you, master," Richard said like a prayer.

*What Sue Generous and I Talked About

"You're traveling around with a famous writer."

"Yes," I said.

"I loved *Revenge of the Lawn* and *The Hawkline Monster*."

"Me, too. And *Watermelon Sugar*."

"Yeah."

"I like the poems too, if less so. Richard was a favorite writer of mine before we became friends."

"Wow. That must be kinda thrilling."

"It is."

"He's an interesting man."

"That he is."

"I thought he was dead."

"___"

"I said, I thought he was dead."

"—."

"Jack?"

"Um, no, the rumors of his death…"

"Ha. He looks good. He must be, what?'

"He's as old as his hair and slightly older than his teeth."

"Right."

"He's a warm conversationalist and a great Father Confessor."

"He seems to like you a lot."

"You think?"

"Yes, I do."

"Hm."

"I think I do too."

"!"

"Don't blanch."

"No, I'm not, I, I don't know what to say."

"You don't like me?"

"I do. Much. Mucho."

"Ok, then."

"You're delicious—your skin—"

"And you're a brown-eyed handsome man."

"I've never been called handsome before."

"Honestly. What, have you been a monk?"

"No, I get cute. I just get cute."

"Come hither, brown-eyed handsome man. Kiss me."

*And When She Came She Said My Name

This seems like a rerun, this twin bed sex scene, this near-orgy. But, bear with me. This is the story's last sex for a while. This Albuquerque sex. This generous Generous sex.

So, with me, savor it. Let's linger.

On twin beds in a shadowy room, halflit by the neon through the curtaincrack.

Ahem.

O Sue, of the cup-sized breasts and slender girlish waist! How lovely you were and are, still here with me, in memory, in memory. And sly tattoos like maps to her verdant, secret places. Sue's clues.

But it was not Love. Yet, I find as I write this down, a tenderness in me for that womanchild in Albuquerque, Sue of the Sheets, Sue of The Frontier, Sue, my own Gelsomina.

And, afterwards, she laid her blinding blond head on my shoulder and we slept like lovers have slept for eons, space travelers, dreamers.

And I slept the sleep water-lilies know.

In the morning the women left early for their own apartments and jobs. Left us with deep kisses and promises, almost as deep.

We, Richard and I, smiled at each other, Merlin's smile, the one that says, ah, life, ah, humanity. The smile that recognizes the impermanence at the heart of the universe and revels in it nonetheless.

*Phone Calls

Norm says: "I can't believe you just took to the road like that. Is this a new and improved Jack.? Jack-lite? Did you call Vita?"

Vita says: "I'm ok. I'm ok. Where are you?"

My sister, Joy, says, "You fuckhead. You can't just leave."

My brother, Lark, says, "A drunk is driving through the city and his car is weaving violently all over the road. A cop pulls him over and asks, 'Where have you been?'

'I've been to the pub,' slurs the drunk.

'Well,' says the cop, 'it looks like you've had quite a few.'

'I did alright,' the drunk says with a smile.

'Did you know,' says the cop, standing straight and folding his arms, 'that a few intersections back, your wife fell out of your car?'

'Oh, thank heavens,' sighs the drunk. 'For a minute there, I thought I'd gone deaf.'"

And Lark hung up. Even if you call him, my brother speaks only in jokes. How do you answer him? You laugh. You only laugh.

*We Decide To Spend One More Day in Albuquerque

"Let's stay one more day in Albuquerque."

"Ok."

***Over Breakfast**

"The number 100," Richard said.

"What about it?"

"It's mystical, especially here in modernity."

"How so?"

"The number of lines a poem should not exceed according to Poe."

"Right."

"The number of minutes in a perfect movie according to Richard."

"Ha. The number of miles before you have to pee."

"Now, you've got it."

"The number of pages in a novella."

"The maximum number of people at a party before the host goes nuts, exposes his wife's breasts, kicks in the TV, and starts railing against the Republicans."

"Ha. The...I've lost it."

"The number of days it takes to write a short story."

"Hm."

***Who's Following Us?**

"It's not you, my friend. Me. He's following me."

"Who, Richard? Are you in trouble?"

Richard looked down at the tea stains on his shirt. He sucked in his moustache. His gemlike eyes scanned the room.

"Don't worry about it," he said, at last.

"I have to worry about you, Richard. I—" and there it was. A precipice. "I care about you." I said this as if the day were not a swelling and the trip a delusion.

Richard looked soulful, sweet. The danger that I sometimes saw in his rugged face dissipated.

"I care about you too, Jack. That's why I want you to trust me. Don't worry about it."

I was reminded of the opening of *The Hawkline Monster*. "I can't shoot a man when he's teaching his kid how to ride a horse," the hired assassin, Greer says.

And the second chapter of *The Hawkline Monster* is: Back to San Francisco.

*In the Watermelon Foothills (Watermelon Redux)

We drove out to The Heights, east of the city, because the women had mentioned that it was the prettiest part of Albuquerque. In the foothills of the Sandia Mountains, which intrigued Richard, because Sandia means watermelon. He wanted to believe that there was a Gnostic connection there, linking this affluent white neighborhood to his eccentric little masterpiece, *In Watermelon Sugar*.

What we found, of course, was just a ritzy neighborhood, like many another ritzy neighborhood.

"Albuquerque is a little dull compared to Santa Fe," Richard observed.

We had already covered this but I was used to my ghost's leaky head.

“John Fowles called Santa Fe the prettiest city in the United States,” I told him. “He said something about how it looked from the air, as if it were carved out of the living rock.”

“I reckon,” Richard said, in that way he had of seeming to be present and absent simultaneously.

We sat in the car looking up at the mountain, looking down at the pavement, letting our thoughts drift toward the hazy horizon.

“Let’s eat lunch,” Richard said. He also had a habit of speaking in pronouncements, as if even the most mundane statements had supranatural import. And, perhaps they did.

***Green or Red?**

Green or red?

This, we discovered, was the predominant question in this Southwestern city. Moreso than Democrat or Republican?

Man or woman?

Straight or gay?

Dostoyevsky or Tolstoy?

Charlie Chaplin or Buster Keaton?

Alive or dead?

***Sex He Said**

We picked up the women at 7 pm. They were both at Sue’s

house.

Sue's house was like Sue herself, nothing flashy, but substance there, inner beauty. Grace. Perhaps I was a little in love with Sue. Perhaps I still am.

The women stood at the curb when we pulled up in Richard's beat-up Buick. They looked like visions out of Hollywood's golden era. The sun gathered in their hair like stardust. Their faces were beatific, trembling with terrible prettiness. They were birds of paradise.

I wanted to be back in bed with Sue immediately. And I imagined Richard's thoughts were along similar lines.

They greeted us with overt affection, planting on us big sloppy kisses, as if we were lovers returned from Troy. As if we were lifelong mates.

Ach.

Did they understand our gypsy mission, that our goal was "Further?"

I don't know.

All that night Sue stayed by my side, so that her warmth spread into me like an injection. I turned to her often, she tipped her face upwards, and I kissed her many times.

We went to eat at Barelas Coffee Shop, which Isabel said was more insider than The Frontier. It was south of downtown and it was murky inside and there seemed to be a rubbed-out obscurity to the place, as if someone at some point had tried to erase it.

"That's the mayor's assistant," Isabel said, indicating a foppish young man seated next to a stunning redhead. "She's a model," Isabel continued. "Arm candy. Cuz he's gay."

We looked longer than we should have at the handsome man and his stunning redhead. They weren't that interesting.

After dinner we drove down through Old Town, to the Rio Grande, which runs like a trickle of semen on the western side of the city. We found a place to lie in the grass and the sun going down into the river was like electric icing on a homemade cake. This is what Richard said.

Was it my imagination that Richard kept looking over his shoulder, kept scouring the shadows with his eyes?

A double agent's vigilance.

After about an hour of outdoor snuggling, the heat rising from our bodies like an ethereal mist, Richard spoke what was on all our minds.

"Sex," he said.

Everything was still for a broken moment. And then we were all fumbling with belts and snaps and zippers and shirtsleeves. In August in Albuquerque the heat is like an overcoat—one wants to strip down, to be naked.

Did I say we were through with sex? I did. So, for propriety's sake, I will leave us there in the grass, half unclothed, alabastrine in the moonlight. We leave our lovers here because sometimes reticence is next to godliness, because we were soon to leave these lovely women with everyone's heart slightly wrecked, slightly cracked, and because our story must move on or it will die.

***Shifting Tents**

Shifting Tents (Tense)!
A Sex Romp
Starring
Jack B. Nimble
Richard "I Ain't Dead Yet" Brautigan

Two (count ‘em Two) Beautiful Women!
Heartache! Heartbreak! Love ’em and Leave ’em!
Come One, Come All!

***Slipping Out**

I woke next to Sue on the bed in her bedroom. On her walls were paintings she had done, very interesting oils, with dark, Boschlike faces, twisting in some kind of surprised ecstasy. There were depths to Sue Generous that I would never explore.

I made my way quietly to the bathroom. The morning was just gearing up outside. So far only the opening credits were rolling.

I startled Richard in the bathroom. He was sitting on the toilet, fully clothed, the lid down. He looked like The Thinker, if the Thinker were an aging hippie ghost in dusty western wear seated on a commode.

“I’m glad you’re here,” he said, as if we had called a meeting. “I thought it would be best if we just slipped out.”

“Oh,” I said, and my heart contracted like a snake going back into its hole.

“Lingering would only make it worse.”

“Yes.”

“I’m a little in love with Isabel,” he said.

Ah, Richard. We were so close, you and I, so sympatico.

“Tell me about it,” I said.

So we did. We slunk out of that house into the wavery dawn like a couple of malefactors. And found our way back to our inn, and packed our respective bags, and paid our bill, and slowly eased into our respective cars, and pushed their noses out onto the slab, just as the sun began to shriek.

And behind us a black sedan, a car made of shadow, followed as if in our magnetic field. Its windshield reflected the sun like a blade would.

***Lark Phoned**

"A man goes to a doctor about his constipation. 'I'm stove up,' he says to the medical man. The good doctor gives the man a packet of suppositories and tells him, 'Take these and come back in 3 days if they don't work.' Three days later he appears in the doctor's office and throws the half empty packet of suppositories down on the doctor's desk. He fairly shouts, 'These would do just about as much good if I shoved them up my ass.'" My brother tells me when I call him from the diner where we stopped for lunch.

***Norm, Vita Phoned**

Norm says, "Are you still following that ghost?" I tell him I am. "Well, keep your wits about you, and, listen, old friend, Lovely Vita needs you. I think she may be cracking up."

Lovely Vita answers on the first ring. "Hello, Jack," she

says, somnolently. “Are you still on the road. Ha,” she laughs a mirthless laugh. “Jack on the road.”

“Yes,” I say to her. “That’s funny. Are you ok?”

“As good as a puppet show,” she says.

I let that go by.

“Do you need me to come back? I will, you know.”

“Jack. Sweet Jack. No, no, I have my friends here…”

She trailed off. I didn’t want to ask her straight out about her awful husband, her broke-down marriage. I was a coward. I wasn’t good at facing things.

“I—” I began and I choked.

“Me, too,” Vita said and the line went dead. The buzz in my ear was like underwater silence.

*Joy, Mom Phoned

I called my sister. She told me to call my mother.

I called my mother. She asked me if I’d talked to my sister.

The family merry-go-sorry.

Richard honked his horn. It was time to keep moving.

*We Salute the Transcendental Hermit

Our narrative continued, its chain re-engaging.

Mesita, Laguna, Cebolleta, Acomita. A poem!

Mesita, Laguna, Cebolleta, Acomita.

Grants.

San Rafael, Bluewater, and its carbuncle, Bluewater Lake State Park.

Where did we stop? Where did we have to stop? I could almost see Richard's head light up as if haloed.

Thoreau!

Thoreau, New Mexico. I here salute you. What bit of differentiated somethingness caused you to name your town after the great Transcendental hermit and philosopher, the Man who Invented Outsiderdom, Henry David Thoreau?

Who knows? Who cares?

We stopped early for lunch—a small nondescript diner called something like Mike's or Mick's. Western Omelets made from crow eggs, on toast. Good strong trucker coffee.

And Richard's eyes twinkling as if the spirit world were opening before him. His mind was gone, gone like a cookbook cake. He was writing poems as if he had never died—his head once again full of billows. He was happy.

***And She Lives in Thoreau, New Mexico**

Richard says this about the waitress: "She tries to get things out of men that she can't get because she's not 20 % prettier."

I don't remind him that he is paraphrasing himself, from his collection, *Rommel Drives on Deep into Egypt.*

"She has nice legs," I put in. I was suddenly very aware of

this waitress. She came alive before me as if in Technicolor.

"She does," Richard says.

"And her smile. Her smile is nice."

"It is."

"She has the kind of mouth you want to kiss even if you don't want it to go any further. A kiss-mouth."

"Yes. That's a nice mouth."

"And she lives in Thoreau, New Mexico."

Richard's face became a map of heaven, a constellation, a light and brilliant butterfly around a dusky flower.

***Oh and**

Oh, and I wrote the first poem that I had written in months, on the napkin in the diner while Richard took care of his business in the Little Poet's room.

Not Much of a Goodbye

I wrote on my pillow
a small verse;

Your head
which was here only yesterday

I hope, dear one,
that it has fallen off.

I find, as I look now at that blurry napkin, that I must have been thinking about Sharilyn. Who else?

***Harley Krishna**

At one point midday a motorcyclist careered past me, a roar from Odysseus's Cave, and slowed as he neared Richard. This biker was large, the missing link in oily denim and leather. He had pelt where I had, have prickly heat.

I am from the suburbs. Guys who look like they belong to Hell's Angels scare the pee out of me. And when I saw Richard roll down his window and engage the hairy gentleman on the hog my heart went kachunk. I strained to see what was transpiring. If Richard were in trouble, could I do anything? No. I was, am, a worthless noodle.

The man rode next to Richard's car for a mile or so and then I saw his large head tilt backwards. He was laughing!

And as he sped away he raised his darkened hand in salute.

He racked away, positively Beatified!

***Some Road Metaphors**

The road is a mouth. The road is a doorway. The road is, as we know, a story unfolding, a book moving from chapter to chapter, with the ease of a sleight-of-hand magicman. The road unspools like a film, like Fellini at his surrealistic best, scene bleeds into scene, actor becomes actress becomes roadsign, becomes cactus. There is a postmodern feel to the constantly shifting terrain. And it's all going—where? It's all going toward a denouement, toward the reason, toward the light, the night, the right. Richard is a ghost and Jack is a ghost's companion, and their journey is a journey subversive, "one would have fancied that the genii of romance were illuminating their underground palaces to receive the sons of men," as Jules Verne wrote. But they are not traveling to the heart of things, to the core, they are traveling to the endtimes, to the border, outward outward outward, to the liminal space that will move their lives onward, to a bardo where they will find—what? Where they will seek no more and find—what?

Stendhal said a novel is a mirror traveling along a highway. I say a highway is a novel endlessly disappearing into a mirror.

*Gallup New Mexico and the Sky Looks Like a Sunburn

Gallup, New Mexico and the sky looks like a sunburn. In fact I feel as if I am surrounded by red, red sand, red sky, saxatile red lizards on red rocks, perhaps my sclera are red, rimmed with fatigue and sleeplessness. Red roads leading outward from my iris like wavering lines of electricity from Dr. Frankenstein's magical cybernation.

Gallup, New Mexico, we hardly knew ye. We passed your State Park, your sideroad beckoning to a Navajo Indian Reservation.

We passed your Wendy's and your McDonald's and your Days Inns as if we had seen it all before. Richard never even looked in the rear view mirror, such was his disinterest, his disenchantment, his eagerness to keep moving. And I followed in his wake, a small boat sucked along by curiosity, love and faithfulness.

*Move Move Move

Friends, I sense your impatience. If I were to enumerate our every stop, our every Prefab Inn, our every late-night black-and-white movie pizza delivery evening, you would want to pull your hair out. You have been remarkably uncomplaining and unwearied so far.

In addition, the most divertive, digressive part of the trip was already behind us. We, too, grew impatient and wanted to move move move. So we did and so here we shall.

Arizona Petrified Forest Sun Valley Holbrook Winslow Angeli Winona Flagstaff (no pause even for such a phallocentric city) small town small town small town small town Kingman small town small town Californicate! Needles small town Old Dad Mountains! lots of white space and then the Golden State for real—Barstow! Where we ate in a diner shaped like a streamline trailer. Barstow the small mouth that swallowed us as we swallowed its sweet cheeseburgers, which led us down the alimentary canal into the maw of California!

We soon had to kiss sweet I-40 goodbye lest we find ourselves in the enema portal of the US, Lost Angeles. So, northward on 5, northward to our goal, our oasis, our Satyaloka, our Eden, our

Shangri-la! San Francisco.

Fast forward and we're there. The air seems sweetened by dewfall and the music from Apollo's lyre. The people are all beautiful, men with shoulder length hair and peaceful mien. Women in flowing skirts and with arms tender from loving. Women with honeysuckles between their legs. We were home.

***A Dream of Negritude**

We checked into a hostelry off Market Street. Richard seemed to know the place and carried himself as if he were visiting royalty. No one recognized him.

Once in our room—it was already mid-afternoon—Richard suggested a nap.

"A nap!" he said. "Do you know that every man who sleeps believes in God, Chesterton said."

"Ok," I said. I was a bit fagged.

Richard took the bed farthest from the window, as always. I don't know why. It didn't seem important, but, in retrospect, it seems, well, odd.

I fell into a hole. Inside the hole a mummery was commencing. It involved a black family and their two daughters. I was engaged to the younger, but the elder, a willowy, drink of strong black coffee, drew me like the sirens. Also, there was a younger brother and he was flunking math which was frustrating their overwrought and overemotional father, reducing the large, gentle man to tears. I tried to help—but I was an outsider, an eternal outsider. I didn't understand their music, their food, their family customs, which seemed exotic as an equinoctial. But the older sister, seated across the room from me, her long, slim legs slung over the chair's arm like saddlery, wore a smile like a buttery comeon. Suddenly, the sister and I were in the outer hallway of their apartment building, almost hidden in the obscurity beneath the stairwell. She set herself up next to me like an outer garment. As I ran my hands over her slim, strong frame, her ass a perfect geometry, she sank her tongue in my mouth like a post in a hole. And as heat rose in me like a flu, I heard Richard's voice, intoning, "Neverland, neverland…" and his face floated near me like the Cheshire Cat's. "Damn you, Brautigan," I was trying to say. "Go away!"

And I awoke to find that face over mine, as big as an October moon.

"Wake up," Richard said, gently.

"Oh, I was so close," I said, head muzzy with sleep.

"Who was she?"

"I don't know...she was dreamstuff, fabricated out of my wheezy fantasy. Yet, yet, she was…I don't know."

"Ah," Richard said.

***Dashiell Hammett Food and Fantasia**

"Listen," Richard said, after we had both visited the euphemism and freshened up. "Right around the corner, I think, in an alley, is Hammett's restaurant."

"Hammett's?"

"I don't know the real name of it but it's all set up as homage to the great Pinkerton writer, and across the street from it, marked on the sidewalk, is where Floyd Thursby got his. Let's have dinner there."

"Sure," I said.

The place was John's Grill—on Ellis Street—a place ostensibly, intentionally secreted away. It felt that way anyway. As if we were entering a secret society. A society built around *The Maltese Falcon*.

The service was friendly, with a wink seemingly behind every response.

Richard and I had Jack Lalane's salad—it was hard to draw a straight line from Dashiell Hammett to Jack Lalane, but we let that pass, and large helpings of any kind of seafood. Richard loved anything from the sea. Scallops, sea cucumbers, the slippery inner thighs of mermaids. His plate was a study in oceanography.

Afterwards the waiter—a man named Jack, too—approached us like the gunsel Elisha Cook, Jr. His pose was studied, an actor's.

"Would you stiffs like to see the Falcon Room?"

Richard looked at me with childish delight.

Upstairs we went, following the short waiter, like ducks imprinted on him. He opened an upstairs door and switched on the light. On the wall, beginning immediately on your left as you enter, was (is) a scene-by-scene recreation of the famous Bogart movie, using movie stills. The opening credits were the first still.

The waiter stepped aside, smug in his knowledge that we would appreciate their meticulous display. It was like walking through the movie. And it felt odd, a room whose walls were devoted to one movie, while the vast center of the room went unused. Yet, when we were through it was as if we had seen the marvelous film again—no, as if we had been *in* it. It was difficult to get the hardboiled argot out of our heads.

We wandered out into the San Francisco night, drunk on mystery, drunk on filmdom's necromancy.

The bright lights of the street seemed like klieg lights. The hooker who motioned toward us from her bright doorway seemed like an extra, someone hired for "flavor." Local color.

Richard grinned like a genii. He kept curling his lip, Bogartly.

"C'mon," he said. "I'll have some rotten nights after I've sent you over — but that'll pass."

***San Francisco by the Bay: an Overview**

That time in San Francisco—what was it? two weeks, 10 days, I don't know—is as jumbled in my sensorium as corn blasted before it is all grown up. I was growing up. We are all in the process of growing up—of growing outward if we are clearheaded enough to realize it—and those days in the Golden City were like a final exam.

I will attempt to hit the highlights as I remember them.

We traveled from pillar to post. Pillar was a party here, a pickup there. Post was bookstore heaven, meetings with other writers. Richard was a social animal. At one point I asked him if he were this way in life, and he said, "Nah, man, when I was alive I was one misanthropic sonuvabitch."

I know what you're wondering. Didn't anyone cadge on to the fact that Richard was back after that ignominious gun blast to the face? Back with his weathered but beautiful face intact? That in fact he was back from the dead?

Friends, I cannot explain it. Here and there we created a mild stir. Sometimes someone would stare at Richard as if to say, Hey, there's something different about him, there's something I can't quite put my finger on. And then it would pass and the drinks and the doobies would circulate and everyone would be lost in convivial cloudsmoke.

Then there was the San Francisco thaumaturgy, the laid back I've-seen-it-all, or more correctly, I-will-see-it-all-if-I-keep-my-heart-open. Most of the poets, writers, dreamers we encountered had already survived and witnessed Hendrix chopping down a mountain with the edge of his hand, Miles running the voodoo down, Mailer and Ginsberg and Cal and Abbie levitating the Pentagon, children with their souls tattooed with tie-dye bringing the president to his knees and embarrassing him into ending a dishonorable war. They got hooked at The Hooker's Ball. They were liberated by Art by the Artist's Liberation Front. They'd seen fire and they'd seen rain. They'd seen the bomberdeathplanes turning into butterflies above the Woodstock Nation. They'd been lost in the rain in Juarez, rePOEsed down on Rue Morgue Avenue, heard the electric violin on Desolation Row. They'd played the game existence to the end. They had arrived without traveling. They had slouched toward Bethlehem. They'd turned on, tuned in and dropped OUT. They'd put flowers in gun barrels and seen those barrels curl back in humility. They had taken the acid test and passed. They'd seen Haight turned into Love. They'd freed Huey, eschewed Dewey and sang Louie, Louie. They'd fought in the Battle of People's Park. They'd dug the Diggers, paid their dues at the Free Store, BEEN at the Be-In. They had gone, ah, FURTHER. And the final sumup was: "Let it go. Whatever you do is Beautiful!"

What was one ghost?

*An Exaltation of Poets and a Soap Opera Called Naked Lunch

One afternoon we were in City Lights Bookstore. I was thumbing copies of *Kulchur* and *Toothpaste* and *Unmuzzled Ox* and *Unspeakable Visions of the Individual*. Richard was in the corner with some young co-ed who was looking dewy-eyed and ripe as the old mustachioed wafting spirit was holding forth on, of all things, rifles. This young woman was not interested in rifles. Instead she was hypnotized like a cobra by the swaying, poetic speech of this lofty balladmonger.

Richard was dipping his line in the pool. He was fishing for a blowjob. He was very skilled at this—he had, you might say, a delicate touch on the reel.

Meanwhile, Mr. Ferlinghetti was going through his mail, seated in an old armchair. He and Richard had spoken briefly when we entered.

Now, Mr. Ferlinghetti raised his handsome, bearded face from the figures in his lap. "Richard," he said.

Brautigan did not even break stride. He was off on a mesmerizing screed. He had his fish.

"Richard," Mr. Ferlinghetti spoke a little louder, a smile twining round his face. "I've a letter here from Allen."

Now Richard turned slowly around.

"What's he say?"

"He and Cassady and Gut are playing with The Fugs this weekend and he wants us to get a carload together and drive to New York."

"Ha," Richard says.

I felt as if I were in a timewarp. Nothing made sense. Everything made its own sense. I was outside of sense. A multiple-choice reality.

About this time Michael McClure came in. Richard's concentration was broken.

McClure hugged his old compadre. Michael McClure was almost pretty like a soap-opera star, if the soap opera were called *Naked Lunch.*

"How's tricks, B.?" he asked.

"Can't complain," Richard said, twisting his moustache like a villain in a silent film.

"Whatcha writing?"

"Got a new idea for a novel. Something like *Tokyo-Montana Express* except this trip is between life and death, death and life."

"You're the man to write it."

"You?"

"Got a new play. Want you to read it. It's about Billy the Kid and Jean Harlow. I'm thinking of getting Ray Manzarek—of the Doors, man—to score it."

"Sounds wild."

"Yeah, yeah."

"Hey, I want you to meet someone."

"Michael."

"Jack."

"Jack," Michael McClure said. He looked at me real hard. He was trying to make sure I wasn't Kerouac. Anything could be true. Anything is. The world is our own construction.

Mr. Ferlinghetti looked up. "Do I know you, Jack?" he said.

"I've got some sweet boo," Michael said.

"Let's go," Richard said. He took the hand of the lass at his side. She followed on the leash as if she had no will. Later we found out her name was Estrella and that she wanted more than anything to be a poet. Her poetry stunk but everyone loved her for her muscular sexuality and her tattoos, which were like a Brueghel drawing undulating on an ecdysiast. Some said she came west from the Nation's Capital, riding the wind like a harpie. Some said she simply left her waitressing job in Kansas City when she read "Constantly risking absurdity" in her High School English class. Her age was given as either 18, 24, or 30, depending on which romancer was telling her story. And her story did get told—she ended up married to the editor of *Inhaling Tin*, which featured everyone from Bukowski to McNamara. It was an adventurous publication. She was an adventurous gal.

***Art 101**

Estrella remained with us that whole day, and we ended up in Golden Gate Park, higher than Gilroy's kite. When the sun went down the women—McClure had his own delightful schoolgirl in tow, a buxom redhead named Sweet Melissa, who looked 16—stripped off their clothing and we painted them with magic markers. They looked like The Illustrated Man when we were through, and, friends, it took us a long time to get through. We men, transformed into Park Picassos, celestial limners, lingered over the swell of each breast and buttock, the tangled folk tales of their pubic beards, bent over in our concentration like monks illuminating a manuscript. We were Diebenkorn! We were Fragonard! Schwitters!

"Mmmmmm," they hummed as we drew on their inner thighs. Tendrils from our flowers creeping heavenward. Richard's marker disappeared into the mysteries between Estrella's strapping thighs. McClure imitated his adventurous friend. They drew now inside their women, as their women drew them inside.

Alas, I was odd man out—Mr. Ferlinghetti and I only sketched, only observed. We had not brought our own canvases, though I was allowed to spend quite a bit of time perfecting my approximation of Jacques-Louis David's *The Death of Marat* on the flawless, bulbous left mammary of Sweet Melissa. Her nipple was a spheral stupa. It became poor Marat's wound.

"Mmmrrrnnnggg," they burbled as their Lascaux walls were ornamented with pictures of the kill. The spear in the bison's back!

Finally Richard—it was always Richard who was sensitive to the group zeitgeist—sang out, "Penises, Gentlemen. Penises Out!"

And we did. And that was quite a night in Golden Gate Park.

*Richard Once Said

All girls should have a poem written about them.

*The Bibliotheca RB

One morning I awoke to a lemony light and an empty room. I had a moment of apprehension, thinking that Richard had been called back, or whatever happens which causes him to travel between realms. Then I saw the note stuck to the TV screen with Godknowswhat.

It said: The day is upon us. Meet me in the restaurant.

The restaurant meant the inn's restaurant, and after ablutions I rode down to the lobby to meet my friend for breakfast. Richard was sitting at a table in the middle of the restaurant, the only other patrons a man who looked like Richard Nixon and his Patlike wife.

"Ah," he said when I entered. I was curious what had him so devil-eyed so early.

I dined on scrambled eggs—are they not the same in every hotel restaurant the world over?—and bacon (a rasher!), while Richard sat there stoked on joe, drinking cup after cup. His impatience was evident.

When done he fairly sprang from his chair. "Let's go," he cried.

He had borrowed McClure's car—an old Woody, a ridiculous car, a grand car—and we went tooling across town, dodging cable cars and businessmen on their way to their grey offices and their grey days. Richard was driving as if driving had just been invented by monkeys and taught to him in secret monkey labs.

On Funston Street, Richard finally slowed down and pulled up in front of a storefront, which looked like a housefront. A gabled, gingerbread house, with tilting shutters and a light coating of moss as if applied by pointillism.

"Here!" he said, leaping from the car.

I followed and we stood before the great white door upon which was nailed a quaint sign: The Richard Brautigan Library.

A rainbow over the arched doorway—did our eyes deceive us?—signifying The Door to Zion, more afterdeath cozenage. The rainbow is a bridge between the real and the imaginary, the affirmed and the dreamed, etc.

I smiled and punched his shoulder. He stood fixed to the

sidewalk, all his reckless forward energies now quieted. He was in a sublime reverie—it had come true. He had written a book, a book full of whimsy and fabrication and gramarye, and, as if conjured by the gods of literature, through their omnificent office, it had come true. Poof! The library existed where no such library had existed before!

Richard shuffled forward—was that a tear?—and I followed him inside.

A woman with long black hair—like a fan of dark lakes—sat at the desk in the foyer. She looked up, smiled, and accepted the dead progenitor of her place of employment, the way you or I might accept the appearance of an old friend. She went back to her book, which I noted was Kit Carson's autobiography.

"Ah," Richard said as we stepped into the main room. "It's all here. It all came true," he said, as if he meant the prince had awakened the princess.

"Look at them, all my children," Richard said, spreading his arms wide.

He walked over to one soaring, tilting shelf—the Pisa Bookcase!—and plucked a book off its ledge. It was a book with a crayoned cover that read *Growing Flowers by Candlelight in Hotel Rooms* by Mrs. Charles Fine Adams.

"Ha!" Richard proclaimed.

We spent the better part of the morning just picking up books and showing them to each other, each little tome—mostly handmade, stapled, mimeographed, or self-published—worthy of our exclaiming. We exchanged titles as if we were swapping the best jokes we had ever heard.

Here is just a sampling of The Richard Brautigan Library's best books (you may want to visit to find your own favorites, though one suspects that the titles change constantly as if by witchery—one day's books is not another's):

Pete Moore's Story by Pete Moore

Beowulf II: The Story of Grendel's Father by Anonymous

The University of North Catatonia Book of Acceptable Behavior by Dean R. Moriarty

Dogs Don't Get Sarcasm by Bernard Malamute

Mugwumpery by Lark Partee

Things are Slow Here at the Dotage by Ransom Stoddard

Talk: A Novel in Dialogue by Creole Myers

numerous issues of a magazine called *Kumquat Meringue*

The Boy Who Used Up a Word by Sonny Lemontina

Situations Defined as Real by Elmer Marks

Dinkums and Furfies by Euphonious Moniker

My Armamentarium by Dr. Morton R. Jackknifing

Marble the Laity by Reverend Robert Mucilage

The Good Appendage by Irish Morpheme

Diddy-Wah-Diddy by Schahriah Balthazar

The New Testament by Barjesus

And on and on. Friends, it was, is a treasure trove. A treasure trove of the nearly-forgotten, the detritus of dreamers and fools. An anteroom of Heaven! Noah's threshold! I could have stayed there for days breathing in the effluence of hopeful scriveners, the perfume of—yes!—immortality.

***One Night Richard Had a Date with Janis Joplin**

I knew better than to ask.

*At the Snit Pitchers Another Otherworldly Time Outside of Time

One evening in a bar called Snit Pitchers, Richard, Robert Crumb and I were sitting, Herme's silence over us like a shroud. Crumb was drawing on the placemat, women with impossibly large hips. His concentration was a watchmaker's, a child's.

Crumb was a good guy, kind of shy and intense in a way, a way that was both likeable and frightening.

Richard was humming along with the jukebox that was playing Joplin's "Move Over." The bartender, a large-boned Swede named Jambalaya, was playing chess with a handsome, dark-headed man, who looked vaguely familiar.

There was another Jack there, a friend of Richard's. How many Jacks in a deck?

I kept still, introspection the only kind of spection that felt right. It was oddly relaxing to be in the company of these men, these creative spirits.

The bartender offered a muted, humble "Checkmate." His smile was almost an apology.

The handsome fellow with whom he was playing leaned back. "Damn," the handsome man said, softly. He stood back from the bar, stretched like a bow-string, bending until his backbones cracked. He was gypsy-handsome. He turned and saw Richard.

"Brautigan," he said, coming over, mug in hand.

"I'll be damned," Richard said.

The two men hugged.

"Didn't know you were in town," the handsome man said.

"Damn," I was thinking, I know this guy.

Crumb spotted a woman shooting pool. I swear she had the body proportions he had just sketched out on the tabletop. Perhaps he had been drawing her though I never saw him look up. Crumb rose and headed her way as if he had heard her call. The cry of the hungry archways!

Richard and our new compadre were talking together, heads bowed so that their speech was all but unintelligible, what with the jukebox—now playing "I Won't Leave my Wooden Wife for You, Sugar"—and the barbuzz.

I leaned away, my mind clouded with loneliness. And my thoughts went to her—my erstwhile San Francisco love—Sharilyn. To be in the same city as Sharilyn and not see her seemed—it seemed as if the world were bent on its axis. Yet, I was afraid. I loved her—that was clear to me now—I loved her as I had never loved before. And I had to have her back in my life. It was so clear to me. It was killing me.

Then I realized Richard was speaking to me.

"Jack, Jack," he was saying.

"Sorry," I said.

"Where were you, baby?"

"Gathering lost threads," I said.

"Ah."

"Sorry."

"Forget it. Jack, this is my old running mate, Dick. Dick, Jack."

"Dick, I said.

It was right there. Who this guy was. It was on the table between us, a toad.

"Dick's written the most incredible, mind-fucking novel."

"Richard," the man said, gently.

"True man. It's called—"

"*Been Down so Long*—" I finished, for I suddenly knew this man to be Richard Farina, the wondrous singer/songwriter, who wrote one magisterial book, *Been Down so Long It Looks Like Up to Me*, and then died in a tragic motorcycle accident the night of the book's launch party. A great loss to American Letters.

"You know the book?" Richard asked.

"I do indeed. One of the truly great first novels in American literature."

"Thanks," Richard Farina said. He hid his mouth in his mug.

I didn't know how to broach the subject. I was getting used to nothing making sense. I was getting used to the easy truck between our world and the afterlife. I wanted to ask this mysterious and talented man if he were going to write something else—the tired old world needs more eccentric masterpieces like *Been Down so Long*. The world needs more Richard Farinas. I wanted to ask him if more work were forthcoming. I wanted to ask him if he were still… still…

"Oh, Dick's dead," Richard said.

*But When He Pulled Out His Dulcimer Death Didn't Matter

He said, this is called "Tommy Makem Fantasy."

He blew the blues away. The night sky opened up and showed its undergarments, its worn, frayed starclusters, a vacant ridotto of universal steeliness and love.

*That Was One Night Among Many

That was one night among many. We trekked in Richard's circles, circles which seemed to embrace both the dead and the living, with no prejudice either way. Circles within circles, outer, inner, jinking, maundering, scudding. Most of the time we danced, sang, and chanted, mere mortals, writers and writers' friends, fantasts. It was a word salad, as lively a bunch of conversations as I've ever been part of.

And I was a component, a cog. Not once was I made to feel that I didn't belong. And, humbly, I submit that I held my own. Oh, I could not swap Old English quotes with McClure, or necessarily follow all of Mr. Ferlinghetti's political arguments. But, neither was I as clumsy as a newborn colt.

*There Were Lunches at Enrico's.

There were women. There was always a gaggle of attractive women—made more attractive by their challenging minds and their swagger. Numerous times I found myself in the corner with some beautiful woman's tongue lolling about in my mouth like a sealpup.

I fell in love a hundred times. I had my heart broken a hundred more. And it didn't matter—life was a rich pageant, a clambake, a dance, a parade. Those were good times.

*Carol Doda Daydreams

One day, in the middle of the afternoon, coming out of City Lights Bookstore, Richard arm-in-arm with Mr. Ferlinghetti, talking lowly to each other, we headed across the street and quickly into the startling interior—it was like stepping out of the daylight onto the lunar surface—of Carol Doda's. A brightly lit gift shop greeted us.

The two writers giggled like schoolboys let out to play.

We stumbled through a small door in the back, a door that was nearly obscured, a secret passage!, and through it we entered a darkened strip club. It was as if we had ambled through a time warp.

Women danced on raised platforms all around us. Large mammalia hung in the air like grapes. Women turned their rounded backsides toward us and bent from the waist—it was all there. Gateways. Mr. Ferlinghetti and Richard walked around the place as if it were a casino and they were gamblers in from Atlantic City. They tweaked nipples, slapped asses, and generally acted like men who knew their way around dancing naked women. They were kings of the underworld!

Friends, I was dispirited by this daylight venture into feminine sexuality. Strippers ma(d)ke me sad. I like a naked breast as much as the next man. I don't like it served to me publicly.

And my mind drifted to Sharilyn. And her willowy, nut-brown nakedness. And I was—O torn! O rendered ventricle from ventricle!

*Richard Wanted To Eat at Cho-Cho's

But it was no more. It was not extant. It was dust. Gone the way of all flesh. Well, most flesh.

"How?" our death-defeater asked.

How could he ask how?

It seemed the first and last thing denied to him (us).

*Hung Up

Yet I was haunted. Haunted twice over, for I could not get Sharilyn Chwedyk out of my mind. I had her phone number—I did go to the trouble of finding it—updating it by calling an old number and having a robot tell me the new charmed sequence of digits.

I could just call her. My confidence was high. Of course it was, cavorting with skalds and artisans and devas and the undead and women as fascinating as piratical romance.

And, so one night, after a round of highpowered drinks, and a round of heavy petting with a curvy poet named Rain—she said she was named after Rilke, but more probably she was named after the storm the night she was born inside her parents' gypsy wagon, among the gewgaws and voodoo paraphernalia, among the muumuus and tiedye, among the illgotten pelf and bijou—I recalled the seven symbols which would conjure forth the voice I had been waiting years to hear again.

"Hello?" she said, and I recognized the curlicue on the end of her speech, a little vocal cuspidation that was all hers.

I hung up.

***You Can Never Go Home**

One afternoon—does it seem I was there for an eternity?—yes, it does, time going all wonky and insubstantial—we drove to Richard's old apartment on Mississippi.

Long we stood on the sidewalk gazing up at the three-story house. An unassuming edifice except that it held necromantic meaning for our exanimate hero. Richard was wavering like bad TV reception. I thought I was going to lose him, that he would disappear like a transported Spock.

Then he sighed.

"Virginia," was all he said.

***A Critical Interjection**

"...Brautigan's originality remains. He has looked at what you and I have looked at, but he has seen things that we haven't."

Terence Malley, from *Writers for the 70s: Richard Brautigan*

***Bridges and Crippled Birds**

Back in the hotel that night Richard was looking at me the

way that phony firing squad looked at Dostoyevsky. He had that sad smile again.

"My friend," he began.

I wasn't in the mood: for commiseration, for fellow-feeling, for advice, for calumny, for palm-reading, sooth-saying, tooth-pulling, eraser-chewing, arm-wrestling, or what have you. I gave Richard a look that said all this.

He ignored it.

"My friend," he said again.

I had no choice but to meet his eyes.

"You have other ghosts."

His prescience unnerved me. Had not I said this very thing?

"What's her name?"

"Sharilyn," I said, without volition. Again again again.

"Sharilyn, ah, yes, the one who got away. The one who broke your heart, left you feeling like wounded marble being poured into the architecture of those who make bridges out of crippled birds."

I recognized "Love is Not the Way to Treat a Friend" and told him so.

He seemed confused.

"I thought I just thought of that. You mean I wrote it years ago?"

"When you were alive, yes," I said, mean-spirited. I do not know why I was taking anything out on Richard.

"Call her," he said, after a while.

"I tried."

"You don't have her number?"

"I have it." She was relisted. Which somehow meant purged of me.

"She wasn't home?"

"She was home."

"You heard her voice and hung up?"

He didn't win any prizes for guessing sequentially.

"Try again, damn you."

I looked at every corner of the dim hotel room. Its gloom was like the gloom in the chambers of my heart. The same webby darkness. The same cheap curtains.

"I'll call her," he said.

"You sure as hell will not."

"I'll hold your hand while you call."

*The Telephone Is Like a Two-Hour Old Streetcar Transfer: Or Ten Bergs A-Calving

So I did.

I called her again. Richard sat on his bed with such a look of love on his face that I was once again stout of limb and heart.

"Hello?" The curlicue.

"Shar—ecch—alyn?" The throat clearing in the middle—damn me to hell.

"Jack?" What to read into this simple pronouncement of my name?

"Hi."

"It's been a long time."

"Yes."

"It's been—"

"Yes."

"What are you doing?"

"I'm talking to you on the phone." Sometimes stating the

obvious is the way to the godhead.

"Ha ha." She laughed her Sharilyn laugh, the one that sounds like crystal breaking. The one that goes through me like a laser through smoke.

"Ah, that laugh. I haven't—"

"You always made me laugh, dear man."

She was speaking as if our past were a short story written by a long-dead American writer, one whose work strained hard to become part of the canon, but eventually fell short, and skewed into an oblivion reserved for the near-great, the writers one occasionally comes across in old anthologies and one's literary memory goes, *plink*?

She called me 'Dear Man.'

"I'm in San Francisco."

There was ice forming on the other end. I could hear the bergs a-calving.

"Sharilyn," I said.

"Yes, Jack."

"Would it be possible for us to get together?"

A long pause, the pause before the blade falls and Monsieur Guillotine dies essentially by his own hand.

"Sure," she said.

"Ok."

"When? How long are you here for?"

"Lunch? Tomorrow?"

"Yes," she said. Her voice was motorized. "I'll meet you at that place in Chinatown at 12."

That place in Chinatown. Our place. She might as well have said it.

After I hung up Richard was grinning like a teacher whose prize pupil had just played "Suite Judy Blue Eyes" on a ukulele.

"Well then," he said.

"Yes. Well then."

*Well Then

I was as nervous as a cat. I dressed in my best funkiness—the shirt I was told looked good on me by a number of women, including my mother and sister. The blue shirt.

I was early. I was scared.

I secured a table near the wall—was it our table? I couldn't remember. I didn't want to send the wrong message. I didn't want to send any message. I want(ed) my life from that moment on to be messagefree.

The owner, a man named Edsel, came over. Damned if he didn't remember me. How do they do that?

She walked in—she was so beautiful I thought I was going to faint. That same long-legged stride, the same chocolaty hair, the same scatter of freckles.

And a face of stone.

She approached the table, not exactly looking at me, not exactly avoiding looking at me.

"Sharilyn," I said.

"Hello, Jack."

"It's been a long time."

"Let's not use all the clichés."

I was stung.

"How are you?" I asked. "Or is that a cliché?"

"I'm fine," she said, adjusting her delicious body in her chair.

The waitress came. We ordered. I don't even know what I said. She ordered some kind of vegetarian noodle thing.

"It's good to see you," I said.

"Jack," she admonished, as if I'd already stepped over the line.

"What?"

"What are you doing here?"

"Well, actually, I'm in town with a friend. It's a long story. I, uh, followed a friend here. He's on a kind of odyssey of rediscovery. A kind of journey through the past."

"Uh huh. And, you came along why?"

I looked at her. I was feeling so low I suddenly didn't care.

"Are you worried that I came to see you?"

"Yes, I am," she said, like an attorney who just found justifying precedence.

"I did not," I said. "Oh, I think in the back of my mind you lurked. The back of my mind being a breeding ground for lurkers. I knew I would want to see you once I was in San Francisco. I think I knew that."

"Did you assume I was still single, still alone, still free to see you?"

"What's the problem, Sharilyn?"

"I just didn't need this right now."

"Then why did you agree to see me."

"I thought I owed you that much."

"Thanks. Thanks for paying all your debts."

"You're so bitter."

"Sure, I'm bitter. You cut me off like a—a—gangrenous finger."

"Still the poet."

"You're not? Did you give up everything?"

She paused now. She considered.

"I'm different, Jack. You don't know me. I've been through some things. I'm just different—not the silly, younger woman you seduced."

"I seduced." I said it like an oath.

The food arrived. I pushed my plate aside.

"I seduced," I repeated.

"Oh, you know what I mean. Our getting together—it was so headlong, so futile and insincere."

"Jesus."

"Don't be angry—"

"Fuck it, Sharilyn. I thought—I don't know what I thought—why is the past so poisonous? Not just for you—why is it such a dead tail for so many women? I swear I do not get it—I don't even care to get it. It's not maturity on your part—it's just emotional sloppiness. Emotional gaming. I don't care. I just don't give a damn."

I said all this in a fury of uncorked emotions. Pandora's Bag, once opened, cannot be controlled. Love squelched quickly becomes unctuous odium. Sharilyn sat there with a composure that was belittling and fascistic.

I took a twenty from my wallet and placed it on the table.

"Fuck it and fuck you," I said, and I left the place.

Once outside my knees turned to water. My steps were unsure. Somehow I made it up the street to the corner where I hailed a cab.

In the dim backseat of the cab I burst into tears.

The Iranian driver turned his radio up.

*Meanwhile Richard Visits His Daughter

While I was ripping open my metaphorical chest with my metaphorical sharpened talons in a restaurant in Chinatown Richard went to see Ianthe. She had grown into a beautiful young woman and Richard was rightly proud. Afterwards he told me, "Jeez, she looks like a cake prepared in the Empyrean ovens by the ghosts of all chefs past."

"I imagine she was quite surprised—" here I was up against it again— "to, you know, find you alive again."

"Hm," Richard said. "That didn't come up."

*The Final Phone Calls of The Following

(1) My sister, Joy, said, "When are you heading home? Mom wants to know. I personally don't care." And she laughed. "Soon," I said. "You sound sad," she said. "As sad as if steering toward dim eternity," I said.

(2) "Joy's worried about you," my mother said.
"I'm heading home," I said.

(2 ½) I did not call Eddie. I had lost Eddie. How sad, to lose the living.

(3) "Shit," Norm said. "Where the hell are you?"

"San Francisco, I told you," I told him.

"Shit," he said again.

"Look. I've seen Sharilyn again—"

"Shit," he said, before I could even finish.

"—and that's over. Dead. Like the dead. Over—dead as a

pharaoh, dead as Chelsea, dead as—uh—Morpheus' imaginings—"

"You don't know," he said.

My heart froze.

"Vita slit her wrists."

"Oh, fuck, oh fuck me, fuck..."

"Jack, Jack..."

"Oh fuck me, fuck..."

"She was in love with you, you shitheel. You knew it—" He was crying.

Lovely Vita in love with me? Impossible. Absurd.

"She left you a note." Norm was sobbing like a travailing woman.

"Oh Vita," I cried.

"She's in bad—she's critical—I don't know what they call it—they don't expect—"

"She's not dead?" I fairly screamed.

"She's as good as," Norm said.

"I'll be back there tonight," I said and hung up.

My chest exploded. My heart imploded. The world was a place of malefaction and monkeys. Everything was tainted, every damn thing exposed as sham and baleful machinations. The darkness closed in around me.

Was it possible Vita could die? That her beauty could be extinguished like a guttering flame?

Of course it was. People die. Good people. Clean-favored people.

Humans are as fragile as rose petals, as ephemeral as seadogs.They just die and then they are gone. It's the world's worst magic trick. And it's not good figuring out how it does it.

(4) "Three buddies die together in a car crash," Lark says. "They get to the pearly gates and St. Peter meets them there. He asks each man in his turn what he would like people to say over him in his casket.

The first guys says, 'I would like them to say that I was a great doctor and a fine family man.'

The second guy says, 'I would like them to say that I was a wonderful teacher who made a difference in many people's lives.'

The third guy thinks a minute and he says, 'I would like them to say LOOK! HE'S MOVING!'"

And the phone went dead.

Dead.

*In Washington Square Park the Rainbow Is Implied

I saw Sharilyn one more time. I ran into her in City Lights as Richard and I were leaving, heading to Green Apple Books to hear Diane DiPrima read. It was our last day in the city—I had told Richard I was needed back home. Richard and Sharilyn eyed each other. Sharilyn seemed discomfited by the dead poet. Richard was making assessments—he knew the score, of course.

"Please," she said.

"What?" I said.

"Can you meet me tomorrow?"

"When?"

Would one more day matter to the dying? My mind was bedraggled with nightmare images of Lovely Vita white as milk, her lifeblood ebbing away, soaking her bed, the floor.

"In the morning, in the park?"

I could and I said I could. Richard looked at me. I couldn't tell if he was disappointed in me or if it was just worldweight in his eyes. The knowledge that love dies, that people separate, and, in his case, the knowledge of what happens after you die. A secret he told me he could never tell. "Sorry," he said. "I'm not allowed to let on what happens after the final click. Ok?"

So, there I stood on a slight rise, a grassy knoll—the same one she and I had made love on, centuries ago, back in the days when mouths kissed in the ashes of Pompeii. She walked toward me in a flowered dress, just sheer enough to show off her perfect, taper-shaped legs. Richard stood a ways off, under an oak tree, talking to a dog, in dog language.

"Jack," she said, and embraced me. Her eyes were, are grey.

I feigned looking past her into the near distance.

"I just couldn't let you go back home with that memory of me."

"Ok," I said. "Are you fixing to make a better one?"

"I hope so," she said. And she stepped upwards slightly—it was awkward on a slope—and she put her warm lips on mine. For a moment I was almost transported. Her sweet tongue touched my lips and retreated. It was a lingering kiss—she wanted to make an impression after all—but, friends, it was the kiss of a dead woman.

She backed away, a smile on her pretty face. Her freckles danced.

"Goodbye, Sharilyn," I said.

She looked at me as if she couldn't quite figure me out.

"Ok, Jack," she said. "Ok."

And she walked away.

***Richard near the End**

Richard came toward me, his face a mask of concern, of warm fellow-feeling. He melted my heart, Richard did.

He quietly put his large arms around me and pulled me against his chest.

He smelled of sweat and patchouli and dust.

And a little of gravecloth.

He placed a hand on my cheek.

"That's all," he said.

I looked at him as if I didn't understand. I understood all too well. He was leaving too.

"We came as far as we could, Jack. Did we come for nothing?"

It was the question I was asking myself.

"No," I said.

"Good," he said.

A shadow passed by at the edge of sight. A dark awareness.

"Goodbye, Jack," Richard Brautigan's ghost said to me. "Goodbye, dear friend."

"Goodbye, Richard. I won't forget all you've done for me."

At the bottom of the hill, on the roadway, shadows melded into corporeal finitude. The dead called to the dead.

***A Parenthetical Possibility and Antepenultimate Roadsong**

(It is said, in the ways of myth and ode,
that while Vita lay, bound like Ulysses,
swaddled wrists, cradled on wrinkled, hospital sheets,
surrounded by light, seemingly made of light,
she was visited by a vision. This
is from her mouth by way of other mouths, on
and on,
and, as such, may have been embellished, embroidered,
rewrit, reorganized, retooled,
and basically lied about.
But it goes like this:
Vita said, I drifted in and out of consciousness,
a packet of discommoded energies,
not knowing the sky from the earth,
the ceiling from the floor,
right from wrong, live from Memorex,
"Purple Haze" from "Foxy Lady,"
salvation from damnation,
exanimate from extant,
dreaming dreams the mermaids dream,
and I awoke to a bright stream of rays through
the hospitals semi-sheer drapery,
and hovering over the end of my bed,
suspended like a truant,
beatific and beautiful,
was a white bird,
a large, white bird,
and its face was the face of old wisdom, a cowboy's face,

which I immediately recognized

as the face of Jack's friend, Richard.

Nothing was said, certainly not by me, and the vision kept its own

etc. But it's smile was as reassuring as

faith. It was—and I don't know of another word for it—it was an ancient smile.

And I knew then that I would

return to the land of the living. That there was where I was meant to be.

And that I would know happiness.

Some happiness, some amount of happiness, at least that, for total happiness is vouchsafed

no one.

This is what Vita told.

And it has been handed down ever since,

burnished until it is as solid as a pine bridge.

It would become the basis for Jack's greatest poem, the one that made

his reputation, "Vita and the Swan,"

perhaps the most honest and bone-deep exploration of

death since "Thanatopsis."

Whether one believes it or not is immaterial.

Vita lives. There is that which is not-death. Which is testament enough.)

*The Penultimate Blues (A Final Study in Gone)

I was bereft.

I told you this was a tragedy.

I would never allow another woman into my life.

I stood on that small rise, a tumulus now, and saw the horizon and the empty Bay and I only wanted to cry for the world's weary wobbling.

Richard smiled a sad smile.

He was holding out his hand. I could barely see him through my tears.

In his upturned palm was a small, queer paperback. *Please Plant this Book.*

Inside were seed packets and poems.

I knew what this was. It was one of Richard's rarest books, an early, whimsical tilt at the windmills of publishing. Its seeds were all still intact, small life-giving bombs.

Richard leaned over and embraced me clumsily.

Then he turned and walked away toward the Bay.

His duster flapped in the breeze. For the life of me it looked as if he were a large, ungainly bird, ready to take flight.

Richard walked toward the black car. You're ahead of me—you already know it's a hearse, a Black Maria.

The man driving the hearse was not a man. He stood next to the driver's door, a mere servant. A batman of the higher (and lower) powers.

At the bottom of the hill, on the roadway, shadows melded into corporeal finitude. The dead called to the dead.

Richard turned back once. It was the smile I knew so well, the non-smile smile. The world-sadness, the endtimes grin.

He half-raised a hand.

But he was already evanescing, like dew. I could see through his half-raised arm. I could see the hippies behind him, the rainbow.

Then his outline began to waver, like TV reception when you turn on a large appliance. Soon, he was barely a human figure.

I watched Richard turning to smoke and I knew that this was it. He turned back toward the waiting car and as he strolled down the prominence he vanished. I did not see the car or the driver evaporate but they were gone, too. It was over.

I was no longer haunted.

The world was a place of Herods and angels, oblivion ha-has, and possibility. A place of sedans as black as the helmsman's bark of old that ferried to Hell the dead.

*What I Don't Know Could Fill a Book

This is that book.

The black car that followed us like a flock of crows. It came for Richard because Richard had transgressed. He had ruptured the veil. In so doing did he create a fissure that somehow ensnared my sweet Vita? Was the separating pall so thin that Vita saw how easy it would be to walk through it? No. I don't know. Her death became mixed up with Richard's non-death.

I was not there when Vita died. I did attend her funeral, which was as sad as doom. Absurd, but I expected Richard to be there. I could (can) not handle Vita gone.

Vita, who was sweet like the rain. Vita, who was lovely as a rill. Vita, who was in love with me. Vita who was.

Vita was. Is.

Epilogue

A Visit from R. B.

Jack Morton was in the upstairs room, the room with his computer, the quiet room, they called it. He was reviewing a book for *The Commercial Appeal* — a new biography of John Berryman, one of Jack's favorite poets. Jack was, is a poet, who sometimes reviews. At the moment the doorbell rang, Jack was not actually writing, he was gathering wool, enjoying the way the wind soughed into the room, lifting the chintz curtains, rustling through the refractory pile of poems he had printed out in the last week.

His wife, Sandy, was in the bathroom with Grace, sharing the bath time as if she enjoyed it as much as their 3 year old. Sandy was able to pay that kind of attention to life, a gift Jack often wished he possessed. He could hear their burbling voices, occasional risibility, and the sloshing of the water. A not unpleasant background noise.

Jack reluctantly rose from his desk. He stretched, taking his time. The bell rang one more time. Jack could not imagine who would call at 8 o'clock at night.

He could see the figure through the semi-opaque glass of their front door. Street-person, he immediately surmised. This area of town—a gentrified old neighborhood, which represented bohemian life in Memphis, Tennessee, where Jack had come to live—had its share of homeless almsmen.

Jack opened the door wearing an expression that could easily shift to annoyance or magnanimity, a flexible face is what he offered the stranger on the stoop. And then a sad smile.

The man was obviously homeless—old, tattered raincoat, soiled trousers underneath, tennis shoes half on, half off his feet, shoes that seemingly belonged to someone else. In addition, the hard carapace one gains from outdoor living. And he had the smell of earth about him. He could be Ian Anderson gone to seed. He could be Methuselah.

There was a feathery mist falling on Central Avenue.

"Yes?" Jack finally offered.

"I'm very hungry," the man said.

There was something disturbingly familiar about his weathered, vaquero face. His scudded whiskers made him look a little like Gabby Hayes.

"Um, hold on," Jack said and started to close the door, stalling for time.

"Too many lifetimes like this one, eh?" the stranger now said.

It sent an icicle straight down Jack's spine.

"Yes," Jack agreed.

"You would have given me food, right?"

"Well, sure," Jack said, not sure at all.

"You're a grown man, a good man."

"Thank you," Jack said.

"You like Memphis?" the man now asked, as if he were a real-estate agent.

"I do," Jack said. "We moved here—"

"Yes," the man said.

Now Jack said something that came from that part of the brain which goes on without us, the part with which we dream—or write.

He said, "I am summoned by a door, but forgotten by the knock."

The man smiled.

"There you go, Jack," he said. "That's my Jack."

"Richard?" Jack whispered.

The man put a hand to his mustache, about which he was seemingly proud. He petted it as if it were a small animal come to rest on his face.

"It's not my time, is it, Richard?" Jack asked, still keeping his voice low.

"No, no, Jack. I had this small window of opportunity and couldn't resist. Even now I am gone."

A silence now came between them, in which Jack could swear he heard the mist falling, like voices of untold multitudes.

"Ok," the wayfarer said.

When Jack went back upstairs, Sandy called to him.

"Who was that, Hon?"

"No one," Jack said. "A ghost."

Jack sat back down at his keyboard. He was absentmindedly fingering the plastic wrapping on his copy of *Please Plant this Book*, which he kept on his desk as a kind of talisman. After a time, something new occurred to Jack. While he loved poetry—it sustained him as nothing except parenting could—he now saw large blocks of prose, like building bricks, stretching out before him on the scrim before his eyes.

Jack had a story to tell and he now saw that he had the means to tell it.

Jack drew up a clean, white, new document.

He wanted to fill it from side to side, like wreathing the day with the tattered figures of night.

And the first word Jack typed was the smallest: I.

Richard and Ianthe

Richard Brautigan took his daughter
downtown to a bookstore
where he hung around talking books
while she followed a cat down
some winding stairs.
Below there was poetry
enough to make your head ache.
At the end of the afternoon they had
ice cream and then went home to
their apartment above the Jefferson Airplane.

Sources

Writers for the Seventies: Richard Brautigan by Terence Malley
Downstream from Trout Fishing in America by Keith Abbott
You Can't Catch Death: A Daughter's Memoir by Ianthe Brautigan
The Beat Generation in San Francisco by Bill Morgan
San Francisco in the Sixties edited by George Perry

These Websites:
http://www.riza.com/richard/bio.shtml
http://www.riza.com/richard/
http://empirezine.com/spotlight/brautigan/brau-intro.htm
http://www.litkicks.com/BeatPages/page.jsp?what=RichardBrautigan * brooklyn
http://www.rooknet.com/beatpage/writers/brautigan.html

and, of course, the books of Richard Brautigan

Acknowledgments

These pieces appeared elsewhere:

"For Sharilyn, Because it Went by so Fast" as "For Kim Because it Went by so Fast" in Muse Apprentice Guild & Dead Mule

"S Again (Exuviae) " as "A Again (Exuviae)" in Comfusion Review

Also, part of this appeared, in somewhat different form, as they say, in *Southern Voices*, ed. by David Tankersley.

And, a portion of this originally appeared in *turnrow,* and then won the Plan B Press Beat Writing Contest and was published by them as a chapbook.

Many of the chapter titles, and most of the spirit of this book, come from Richard Brautigan's singular work, part conjuration and part ticky-tack. The joke about the two popes I first heard, I believe, from Am Hempel.

Some additional thank yous:

Elea Carey for her love and for her knowledge of the country called America west of the Big Muddy, Steve Stern, Ward Abel, Dan Wickett who is so supportive of writers that you would think books still matter, Doug Hoekstra, Rebecca, Debra Jackson (my comely cousin), Ray Succre, Ben Tanzer, Meg Pokrass, Uncle Terry, Grace, Ashley, Selah, Mark Hendren, Sue Williams, Joe Taylor, Paul Hunter, Marly Youmans, Steven Allenmay at Plan B Press, the good folks at *turnrow*, and to my family, past and present, here and gone.

Author's photo: Chloe Mesler

COREY MESLER purports to be the author of the preceding. His asseveration is crooked at best. He is also a known prevaricator making this whole enterprise fictional, fictional, fictional. When his novel, *Talk*, received kind words from some of his heroes, like Miles Gibson, David Markson, Steve Stern, Frederick Barthelme, etc, he could only shake his head and mutter, "O if God should punish men according to what they deserve, He would not leave on the back of the Earth so much as a beast." Corey now lives somewhere between Memphis and Death..

"I do not want to achieve immortality through my work. I want to achieve immortality by not dying."
Woody Allen

www.ingramcontent.com/pod-product-compliance
Lightning Source LLC
LaVergne TN
LVHW090935080826
845145LV00003B/761

* 9 7 8 1 6 0 4 8 9 0 4 7 1 *